The Plug of Lil Mexico 2

Lock Down Publications and Ca$h
Presents
The Plug of Lil Mexico 2
A Novel by *Chris Green*

The Plug of Lil Mexico 2

Lock Down Publications
P.O. Box 944
Stockbridge, Ga 30281

Visit our website @
www.lockdownpublications.com

Lock Down Publications
Like our page on Facebook: Lock Down Publications @
www.facebook.com/lockdownpublications.ldp

Book interior design by: **Shawn Walker**
Edited by: **Kiera Northington**

Chris Green

Stay Connected with Us!

Text **LOCKDOWN** to 22828 to stay up-to-date with new re-
leases, sneak peaks, contests and more…

Thank you!

Submission Guideline

Submit the first three chapters of your completed manuscript to ldpsubmissions@gmail.com, subject line: Your book's title. The manuscript must be in a .doc file and sent as an attachment. Document should be in Times New Roman, double spaced and in size 12 font. Also, provide your synopsis and full contact information. If sending multiple submissions, they must each be in a separate email.

Have a story but no way to send it electronically? You can still submit to LDP/Ca$h Presents. Send in the first three chapters, written or typed, of your completed manuscript to:

LDP: Submissions Dept
Po Box 944
Stockbridge, Ga 30281

DO NOT send original manuscript. Must be a duplicate.

Provide your synopsis and a cover letter containing your full contact information.

Thanks for considering LDP and Ca$h Presents.

Grady Memorial Hospital

Atlanta, GA

Smokey

I was opening my eyes to everyone standing in a hospital room around my best, as if it was my funeral. Not only did it throw me in a panic, but I was reminded of the incident that just occurred when I tried my best to lift up in the bed.

"Shittt!" I grunted in pain, trying to shake the sharp aggravation on my flesh.

An attempt was just made on my life, not just mine. Family, Keith for the second time, and the realization that we weren't protected like I thought, crept to the center of my brain.

"Smokey, are you okay, sweetie?" Simone leaned down to my right side, rubbing my cheekbone.

Her beautiful face stressed worry, her vibration, attitude. It was all connecting to me as if I'd known her my entire life. I smelled sincerity all over her, and it was different to actually see a woman remain by my side after a sticky situation like mine. I was more than grateful.

"I think I'm okay, where is everybody? Did Keith get hurt?" My mind instantly went to worrying about my dawg.

"Keith's fine, Smokey, he went to make a quick call. You were just shot twice and lost a lot of blood. We need to be making sure you're okay," she stated with sympathy that reminded me of my mother.

"I tried to kill all of them muthafuckas! I couldn't even see a face, boss! Coolio spoke with anger drizzling off his tone.

His Prada button-down was open, his Glock was showing on the side of his hip, and he couldn't stop walking around, so I knew the mental side was all the way in his vision. I knew he could shake some shit quicker than an earthquake, but what was the reason for going in the ocean's water without knowing which prey is stressing my demise for their daily schedule. I didn't want to fight a ghost, so I eased him immediately.

"And don't think you did anything wrong. As long as you clap back, they know dying is close by their side as well. We have to be smart, and move off smiles, and humbleness. We gone act like this ain't never happened and look for our babies on the low. We have to much at risk, so you gotta trust me on this one. Whoever did this might as well shoot a needle full of poison. Ya feel me?" I gave him a serious stare down.

"Understood." He clasped his hands, lowering his head with a long sigh.

His heart was always in the right spot, but it was attached to emotion, which could cause us to get killed in the streets. I wasn't with that shit. If we were gonna stand for what we were doing, we were about to stand for eternity. It was all the way, or none.

"Listen, nothing is about to stop us from getting this predicament over with Rhestay. We have no room for slips. We have to eat in this process, so I'm damn sho not about to fumble another man's money that's gonna have to pay me in the end. Blue was the reason the entire movement began, so fucking up the ball was out the window when I agreed to handle this business for him. We can't lose, but we have to stay tight. Call Pauline, and Janet. Make them get the order for the road ready, we pushing more security on the blocks we control, and taking the loot, the same day the runners close down shop. If they see anything strange, tell em to kill and we will think of what to do later."

Right when I finished speaking my peace to a few of my men, and Coolio. Keith walked back into the room with Felipe right in his tracks. He was silent, no emotion. He came to stand beside me, folding his arms, and I knew he only wanted to run wild. I just wasn't about to give the green light yet.

"Are you good, my nigga? You fucked me up there for a minute." Keith tapped my leg lightly, smirking.

"Come on, man, I was ready to go when I opened my eyes. You can bet we investing into some more shooters before I leave out of this building. Is all still set for us cranking up this weekend?"

"I'm not sure, Blue is raging, and he's tired of disrespect shots that doesn't have an address to answer back. He wants war with everyone, and thinks we need to lay low. My mind is saying keep the paper on the road, but move a lil more discreet, bro. We were all at stake with this shit. He shook his head with disappointment.

"So, you mean to tell me y'all know it's people out here trying to kill y'all, and partying in public is what y'all do, while inviting the entire to city to give up your exact location. Why even risk each other. Money has never been that important." Simone looked at us both with a curious gaze.

I knew what she was saying was more than true, but the reality of what we had going was pushing her action to the left. We had the hold on making a nasty profit from our product, and I wasn't going to leave the clientele, nor the hustlers lost without giving them a heads up. We still had to eat.

"Look, Simone. I respect your mind, love, and even the fact you stayed down here after this confusing night, but I'm a hustler. It's a job that chose me, and switching it up would mean me, closing my survival. I wouldn't do that for anyone. Not even myself," I said, with the uncut response from the heart.

I could tell that my answer bothered her, but her calm beauty told me that she respected my beliefs. I needed a strong individual like her around when things got blurry, but I had to see exactly what her true intentions were for me. Until then, I was executing for any problem presented.

"Well, we're gonna have to check in with Blue before we go out on that road, plus having shots I'm the streets only makes food for cops to live off. We gotta kill if necessary, not because of anger just for seeing the nigga in the open. I'm calling our best shooters in for double shifts. We have to move this shit quick, pay Rhestay, and stack enough money to feed our next fifteen generations." Keith folded his arms with that usual look of confidence.

"I'm riding behind you no matter what ditch we gotta crawl through. In order to run the city, we gotta make sure the people have a chance at trying to stop us. After they fail. We toast champagne, and smile. I'm with it." I closed my eyes to feel my body ease.

Simone's hand touched my shoulder.

"I'll be right here until you rest up. Right here."

Letting my eyes shut for a second too long, whatever meds in the vein of my right arm, drifted me right to sleep.

Chapter 1

Keith

I had to kick back for a second at the hospital to get my thoughts aligned. Something I hadn't done in forever. My mind had been incarcerated to a drug selling mentality, and it almost seemed like the end of the world when I was blocked away from that. I made attempts to talk to my uncle across the payphone line, but he refused to speak. I knew brutal criticism was heading my way. If failure became attached to any task he placed in play, he bashed the fuck out of me. Smokey would probably receive a double portion for making wrongs at the beginning of our ties.

Making my way back inside the hospital, I brushed up against a man accidentally. The nigga damn near appeared out of nowhere.

"Excuse me." I couldn't even get the full apology out and by the time I tried, he was gone.

Brushing that shit from my mind, I made my way back upstairs to pick up Smokey. He had to leave the hospital, and nothing, or anyone, was gonna change his mind about that.

***

Blue's Home

Five hours later, after finally being released from the dragging ass medical clinic, we had finally arrived at the driveway of my uncle's crib. I could already hear the venting vibrating through his walls.

"You ready?" I looked at Smokey, trying to push him first.

"Nigga why you asking that like we ain't sitting right in the parking area? We damn sho ain't meeting in the grass."

Smirking from the remark, I shrugged the care from my attitude, and got out. Helping Smokey out the passenger side, he balanced on the crutches, with me assisting him straight inside. Upon entering Blue's front door, a few unknown faces stood against the wall, in the bottom level hall corridor. Me and Smokey paused for a second. I was never used to seeing people I didn't know personally in the folds of his pad.

"Who the fuck are you two weird ass niggas?" I shot them a nasty mug.

Both men were obviously white, and all business-like, with their posture speaking for them.

Moving past them to the living room area, I found my uncle in deep conversation with a bald black man that was wearing an all-black trench coat. His plain button-down was off-setting his white slacks. He wore black boots that favored a pair from a military assignment in Iraq.

They immediately cut the conversation when he glanced back, noticing me and my company. Blue patted his shoulder, quickly allowing him to exit without saying one single word to me. I didn't understand yet, but it took shit time to play out in order to get certain shit.

Helping Smokey sit down to rest, we waited for my uncle to reappear. It was nearly ten minutes later when I realized he made sure the strange guest exited the property before even holding a conversation about what went wrong.

Blue took a seat on the Italian leather couch across from us, with a look that said maybe even we could be murdered. His first statement was swift and straight to the point.

"I need to know what the fuck happened. I'm critiquing or should I say more of a unique moment on where I'm molding my business. I love you, nephew, but I refuse to let you ruin my business, regardless of how much I love my sister. I won't allow you." His words fell out with a straight face.

Before I even responded, I ran everything back through my head to be sure I kept it thorough as possible. I knew that Blue didn't respect losses, but he didn't respect lies even more. Since I was fourteen, I had been involved in the business ever since my uncle accepted me under his own roof. I was never meant to gain access within the bounds of his business, but after the slight struggle my mother was placed through when I was a teen, he acted as if it was his responsibility to take me in. After I was introduced to his ways, I embraced the game and jumped in headfirst. Now the slips were starting to rise, and that was just something he wasn't used to.

"Blue, it was a fumble that we didn't see. We don't usually have issues where people are trying to kill us after a night inside of a club. We were caught completely off guard. It's really a lost for my answers, but as for excuses, I'm not making any," I replied with much respect.

Standing up from the couch. He sparked a cigar. A small smirk formed on his face, before snatching the small glass statue from the coffee table between us and slinging it forcefully to the wall. I had to turn my face from the small shards of glass that ricocheted our way.

Smokey's face turned up in anger, and I didn't know what was about to come out of his mouth, but it damn sure caught me off guard.

"It was my fault, Blue. I forced Keith to take me out after he stressed about focusing on the business. Don't feed any negativity to him. I deserve it all." He nodded at Blue as if the lie was pure.

For what it was worth, it did have some kind of effect, because Blue sat back down on the couch, exhaling for some patience, but more for the care and well-being of the status we've built.

"What am I supposed to feel if I happen to get the message you are dead, and even worse, more people are dead for our slip-ups. You know what that will do to me, Keith. Smokey hasn't been around us long enough to place an action into your head. This is not you. Smokey, you can't try to claim every problem because if you do, that means you're the problem. I would suggest you worry about perfecting your steps to make this never occur again. Losing your life isn't a part of the mission we have here."

"I do want this Blue, and whoever has laid this plot out for us will feel just like the rest of the ones that have pressure with us."

"I'm hoping so, because this isn't the way my name gets represented. I have calls to make with Rhestay in order for this process to keep pushing. Hustle if you two are going to hustle. "Nothing else," he ordered before walking out of the living room.

Looking over at Smokey, I frowned.

"So, it's all your fault, huh?"

"I mean…sorta, but what the hell was I supposed to do? Allow all the backlash to fall on you? Hell, I was the one that got shot and we both know all this shit is happening because of me. It's time to switch shit up just like Blue said, but I need you to rock with me on the plan."

"A plan? Dog, you freestyle damn near everything you do. Jumping in a pool headfirst should have been your profession, muthafucka!" I laughed, leaning my head back on the couch.

"Yeah, but I'd rather dive in that water headfirst, before I sit back and never jump in at all. Life is about taking chances, and every achievement anybody on this earth has succeeded

14

with, came from taking a risk. We the key, we just have to turn that bitch."

Smokey's theory sat with me for a second, and after processing the ins and outs of it, he made sense. I guess it was more of the fear about losing someone close, the entire operation or even worse, our own lives. It was more to me than just collecting a dollar bill off the next key of coke. It was truly about the family, and Smokey was a part of that now.

"I'm with it, but if we're gonna do this, you have to let me tell you when the wrong shit is being placed into effect. I'm not against you, bro, but we can't keep doing this. I have a few ideas of my own. I just don't need our ideas clashing for wanting to make money. We win without the money. Just with the fact of us still having our lives.

"I understand, bro. It's your car, so you need to drive, cause whatever your decision is, we're going all the way. So, what the hell we about to do?" he asked, impatient to even finish our convo.

"We're gonna do exactly what we need to. Blue will have to understand afterwards. We need to go and talk to Pauline and Janet, like now." I grinned.

He gave a confused gaze, but I could clearly see he was lost on what I had in mind.

"Nigga, I got a bullet took out of me six hours ago. We really gotta go now?"

"Naw, you don't. Just kick it with Blue for a while, and I'll go give Janet and Pauline the run down." I shrugged, heading for the door.

"I'll get a few pain pills out of the medicine cabinet." He rushed to grab for his crutches.

I laughed, knowing he couldn't live if any action would occur without him. That was the same reason I knew no one else could be the perfect grinder to stand beside me.

***

Pauline & Janet's

Smokey

Sliding over to Clayton County, Riverdale area to be exact. Me and Keith stepped out of the car, staring at the crib. I didn't know if we were having the same thoughts because I immediately noticed the police squad car, sitting in the side driveway. Before I could say anything, Keith took the words right out of my mouth.

"Is that a fucking cop car, or maybe I'm just still feeling the bud we smoked from a little earlier?"

"I think that bud you smoked was some bullshit, because I damn sure see the same shit. What the hell are we supposed to do?"

I was damn near tempted to turn around, get in the car, and never enter through the county. The only thing that forced me to remain was the fact I had over two hundred grand in bricks, all in possession of Janet and Pauline's hands. Plus, they were too loyal to just leave, wondering and guessing on what was truly transpiring inside. Instead of me answering the question, I moved calmly to the door as if I belonged there and knocked.

"So… what, we just about to go in here and let the cops know we the brick manufacturers of the city? Maybe we just need to double back later on Keith," he suggested.

"I can't just leave them like this. I at least gotta check."

Knocking on the door, Smokey closed his eyes as if he was just shot, presuming he didn't have a chance to walk off. Shittt, we were in this shit together, so I made a decision for both of us.

We waited patiently for the answer, and when I heard the sound of their adjusting, I prepared myself. Pauline's head peered out from inside, and the laugh she gave me threw me for a mixed vibe.

"Ohh shit, Keith, I didn't know that you were coming to check in today. Hey, Smokey. Y'all come in," she offered, stepping to the side.

I didn't know if we should take her warm embrace as a setup, or if we just going through a phase of confusion, but I guess she caught ahold of the expression our faces and not to mention, we were still standing on the porch like fucking mannequins.

"Are you sure it's okay to enter?" I nearly whispered, cutting my eyes over to the side of the house where the cruiser was sitting.

She looked confused for a minute and burst into another fit of laughter.

"Boy, if y'all don't bring yo ass in this crib, and get off this damn porch."

She walked back inside of the house, leaving me and Smokey in our spots. I didn't want to be tossing confusion on what we needed to do, so I took the initiative and entered first.

The inside was plush, good appliances and great decor, even minty smell lingered in the air. We proceeded to the kitchen where she was sitting with a fully dressed officer at the table. He was black with a low buzz cut. His face never looked up at me and Smokey. He was cleaning a hand pistol, while Pauline sat at the opposite side cutting down a key of cocaine.

"Uhh, is everything okay, Pauline? Why are you cutting open flour in the daytime like this, are you about to throw a cookout or something?" I tossed in the air to see what the hell was going on.

She gave me an aggravated glance, and the male at the table with her finally looked up.

"Flour? Right…" She went back to busting down the brick.

"Is everything okay?" the officer butted in.

"He thinks you're a real cop. You probably should've pulled out your badge by now, or at least flashed a pair of cuffs."

"What? Hell no, man. This is just the costume during the daytime for me, fool. My sister told me she needed some help moving some things. I own my own vans, not to mention, I print labels and IDs, or anything else around this bitch with a stamp in this world as a business label. This just happens to be my latest design." He smirked, holding the collar of the police jacket between his fingers.

Smokey had to kill the entire thought process I had by laughing at the guy with a pointed finger. "What the fuck? How the hell we know this nigga ain't lying?"

"Because I just explained to you that he's my brother, motherfucker, that's why. I don't know what the hell has gotten into your friend Keith, but I've been doing business with you and your uncle since I can remember, and we've never had anyone disrespect this friendship with any deceit yet. So, maybe we need to see if *you're* lying about something, big man." She shot daggers back towards Smokey.

Just from his face balling up, I knew shit was about to get real. The last thing I needed was a fallout between two main pieces of my team. It was already too much going for me to lose my mission at hand, so I ceased the bullshit immediately.

"Whoa, let's just slow down for a second, Smokey. You too, Pauline. We're fam, and that's not how we speak to each other, period. This is literally the only team that we have at the top of our project, and if this goes down shit creek, we're fucked with my uncle. Is that shit understood?" I looked back and forth between them to make sure it didn't crank back up.

"I'll be waiting at home, Pauline, I think this was a bad idea." The man stood from the table to leave.

"No, sit back down. We have business to handle, my friend, so that means leaving is off the fucking agenda for right now." I patted him on the shoulder.

"What the hell is up with the vibe today? You asked me to come up with a way the drugs can be shipped out to the states quickly, without any way for it to be stopped, or seen. I brought something to the table that could make it happen ten times better. We don't need this today. You musta forgot we can keep the little movement going with, or without your help," he stated arrogantly.

I recognized the emotions were really flowing, so I decided just to jump straight to business. Taking off my white Gucci patterned coat, I tossed it over the chair and sat down.

"Listen, we all are here for one reason, and the purpose is self-explanatory. So, my question is, what can you help us do? We have almost eighty kilos that has to be pushed up north, out of this state until we deliver every key. Cincinnati, Carolina, Jersey, Baltimore, and the rest of the white suit states that pisses on top of those. Where do you fit in?" I sat back and listened to what he could tell me.

Standing to his feet, he smiled at Pauline and took the floor.

"Now, my talent only comes once in a lifetime, so most of the people that get into business with me, understand the limitations of my craft. I can't be stopped when it comes to making runs through any state. I have vehicles and tags for every business and agency, downloaded from my computer drive. I can even handle a stop, if necessary, because I have fake lines to call for whatever company we push through the streets at the time. There will be someone to answer that can also give you verification of whatever you need to know. They're experts. I have three different avenues we're gonna use to complete this job within three days."

"Three days? Yeah right, nigga. It took us nearly a week the last time we were on the road, and that ain't including resting and gas breaks. You must be about to do a couple shots of heroin and eat a small bag of raw coffee. Cause if you ain't, that's impossible," Smokey added.

"I don't know, the time limit you're pushing on the package dropping is kind of far-fetched. We can't drive for three days straight!" Pauline folded her arms.

He laughed with a pointed finger in the air, as if we had no ounce of faith.

"That's where you guys are wrong. We're gonna have three teams. One prison transferring van, one delivery truck of Green Farms Trucking Co., and another load delivering from Unique Moving Company. That's thirty keys apiece, and if we use a three-team crew with every truck. Everyone would have an eight-hour driving limit through every city. That allows the last driver exactly eight hours to rest. By the time the rotation switches, a drop would have been completed, and the next driver would have had the full amount of rest to take back the wheel. Within those seventy-two hours, if they keep the pace of what I calculated, they will be entering back through Georgia on the third day, around four in the evening," he explained, looking back at me to see if I caught all of it.

He'd just explained so much that it had my head spinning for whatever answer I needed to provide. The one thing I could say was his theory sounded great, and if it could work, we would have a brand-new foundation on the way we handled our business. Not only would we be able to move the keys quicker, but quieter.

Standing to my feet, I folded my arms, studying him before asking my last question.

"So, what if this doesn't work, the three-day move as you're guessing. Then what?"

"Uh, I'm not guessing. I'm giving you facts, but if you have so much doubt…if it doesn't work, I'll deliver the rest of your packages myself for free." His eyebrow raised as if he was testing my mind now.

I had to respect his talk game, because it sounded more than good, I just couldn't see us taking a loss.

"What's your name?"

"Terry, but everyone calls me Ty."

"Alright, Ty, let's see if this magician trick of yours can pull through. The show is in your hands. What's next?"

"I'll let this beautiful sister of mine take the floor now." He nodded towards Pauline.

She smirked, rolling her eyes at Smokey, and pushed the neatly wrapped key of rewrapped cocaine to the center of the table.

"Wow, I'm surprised I haven't been rejected by the jury yet. Am I actually in charge of having to get this shit across the states? The bitch who's not to be trusted," she complained.

"Take it as an apology for all the bull I've wiped out of my hair. I'll pay for you a butt lick after we handle this." I smiled, waving her off.

"Yeah, you'll be the one doing the licking, muthafucka, the next time this asshole comes in here with his balls tucked in his ass. Now back to business. Do any one of you boys have the necessary tools to play with a few of these?" she asked, pulling a box from under the table.

"Is that a car tire tube?" Smokey asked, trying to get a better look.

"You damn skippy," Pauline shot back.

A smile spread across my face, and it wasn't for the fact of the room making up quicker than a miserable couple on the verge of divorce. It was because the money my family was making was about to increase by the mile, and Pauline and Ty was going to be the ones to thank.

Chapter 2

PoBoy's Mother

1:15 am

Montgomery, Alabama

I had been getting my back fucked out for the past hour, and my craving for killing a motherfucker shot up with every stroke this nigga delivered to my gut. It was the mixture of tortured pleasure, and it was the only way I could get my mind off pulling a trigger for the death of my son, PoBoy.

"Damnn! Sss! You better not stop until I cum!" I warned him as he started to hit a lil harder.

Once I felt that massive orgasm pop out of my pussy, I pushed his ass clean off of me, and caught my breath. It wasn't even the same without Fresno, and the nigga T was the reason for that horror, creeping into my mental each night. It was to the point I had to find a random fuck just to picture my man was back home with me. Not him, and my son was just a memory. Once again for the cause of Miami T.

"Get yo shit and leave. The fuck was nice and if I need you, I'll call," I told my little fling as he tried to coop up in my bed.

This nigga had the nerve the wrap his arm around my neck, whispering in my ear. "I was thinking I could spend a little extra time with you, maybe fix some breakfast, and get our freak on for a little hour or two after."

I reached under my pillow, grabbing my nine, sliding it clean under his chin. I could feel his balls shrivel up into his stomach.

"If you don't want your thoughts on dick plastered to my ceiling, you'll put on your clothes, get the fuck out of my bed and house! Now!" I hissed.

Buddy backpedaled like a dog, falling to the floor. Running out of my bedroom, clothes in hand, he slammed the door behind him. If he was lucky, he would make it out the front door, without my brother's bodyguard mistaking him for a burglar, or rapist. It was a miracle if a stranger stepped foot on our property, but a bigger blessing if they left it alive.

Stepping out of my bed, my home phone rang. Letting the silk sheet fall from my naked body, I answered, truly not trying to even be interrupted at the moment.

"Who is it?"

"Sis, it's me, Chino. Listen, I've come up with a twenty-man crew to take back up to Atlanta with me, to try and exterminate these clowns. All I'm saying is that we have a short window with trying to duck off in these people's area without getting our cover blown. We can't afford for nobody else to die on our watch. We got the money. I'm not understanding what this will do on our benefit," he said through the line like he was fucking nervous.

He was my husband's brother, but lately his actions were showing me the money truly meant more to him, than executions of the muthafuckas that took his own blood away from him. I didn't care who didn't like it. We were gonna either kill Miami T and his entire family or spend our living days until I watched it happen.

"I don't care about risk, or lives, nigga. My fucking son is dead. Your brother was murdered by this man for nothing, Chino, are you listening to yourself?" I wanted to jump through the receiver and slap the fuck out of him.

Walking to my bathroom, I started the shower still listening to the retreating ass words spilling out of his mouth, and I was gonna ensure that it did no good, regardless of what he felt would come from my decision.

"I understand your pain, Stacy. The feeling is nothing none of our own can say they are going through. Especially losing Fresno, and PoBoy. But we have to think smart, before we end up next in line with them."

My heart was unsatisfied, beat down with defeat. I was tired of losing my loved ones. All to the same game that was supposed to kept us fed and protected. it wasn't the same anymore, so in order for me to make my name be remembered, I had to shake the ground, and force people to recognize who we were.

"I don't care about your little pep talk. If we don't step on this shit now. We're gonna die without these muthafuckas even having to pull a trigger. I want a team up there, and I want the tree shook harder until all the leaves are laying under the roots. That's all, Chino." I tossed the cordless phone on the bathroom sink top.

The steam quickly filled up the space, and I didn't hesitate to step in. Once I started to lather the soap against my skin, Fresno's warm hands started to dance around in my imagination as always. His fingertips sliding down my back, warm kisses against my neck. His manhood sliding between my legs. I closed my eyes, feeling the tears ready to cascade down my face. Instead, I replaced it with a smile. It was not for personal joy, but because everyone who caused me pain at this point was gonna pay with their lives. I wouldn't stop until I felt Fresno next to me again.

***

Detective Murray Brown

Chris Green

DeKalb County Jail

Taking my time to ride out towards DeKalb County's housing space, I entered the building. Heading straight for the eighth floor, which was supposed to be for the maximum-security inmates to be held. I didn't like the assignment I was on for today, but it seemed like Chief Williams only wanted the protection of this idiot secured. He wanted to make sure we could build a case on Miami T about a shit load of things I wasn't aware of.

"Hi, Detective Brown. You're here early, aren't you?" a staff member asked me as I headed for the visitation area.

"Yeah, it's just a little dipshit work before the birds get to chirping up my ears. Could you have a few guards bring me inmate Gary Baxter please? I need to speak with him."

"Sure thing, sir."

As she walked off, I sat inside the small room fumbling through an ass of papers. It was beyond my knowledge what all this recent murder was about in the Zone Six area, but ever since Miami T's release, a hellhole for the portal of demons literally formed in the center of our streets. It wasn't a magnificent deed to take the lives of other criminals, but I couldn't say it wasn't a slight helper on the department's behalf. I hated to clean up the nasty mess of a man that had been causing chaos for the city I was supposed to protect with my life, under oath. So, when the pressure came to them, from others just like their kind, I never had empathy for one at disadvantage. Neither did I have mercy on the one's causing the oppression. It was like taking care of two birds with one stone.

Just as I started to get lost in my thoughts, a sheriff opened the visitation room door, and allowed Mr. Baxter to enter. His hands were cuffed, even though he couldn't get past the large plexiglass blocking us away from each other. The side of his face was still badly bruised, and judging from the look on his face, he was stressed beyond his usual limit. I knew a man that was on the verge of cracking, and he was definitely one.

"If it isn't the infamous guy, Gary Baxter. How you holding up, big man?" I smiled as if we were best friends.

"Not too good. You told me I wasn't gonna be in here for more than a few weeks. It's been nearly a month, motherfucker. That wasn't a part of the deal, Murray!" He stressed through clenched teeth like a hungry pitbull.

I laughed, causing his eyes to slant more like the devil's. He was ready to kill me. Lord knows what would have happened if he possessed a gun at the moment. At the end, there was a protocol he had to follow if getting back on the street was anywhere in his agenda. So, I decided to go ahead and break the ice to make sure we were on one accord.

"Listen to me, fuckman! Sit your two-dollar ass down, before I let the real killers in your population make coins out of you." I pointed towards the seat in front of him.

I'm guessing he saw the seriousness in my eyes, and began to calm down, because he slumped down into the chair, looking defeated.

"Now, it's only been twenty-one days Mr. Killer, and the only reason you're still sitting in here is for your own safety. Because, if you were on the streets, you would have probably been found behind an abandoned building. Second, the captain of the department wants you to handle the business agreement of testifying against Miami T inside of a real courtroom, not just over a sheet of paper and recording. We need a physical testimony to make sure we can put this monster away forever. It's the only way we can ensure you'll walk around without a bullseye on your back."

His facial expression drained to my words, and his body slightly leaned forward towards the glass.

"What are you not listening to, Brown? If I do that, it's no point of even leaving from behind this wall. These niggas have avenues around all the blocks I'm around. It's a difference from me snitching on paper, but you're trying to get me to commit suicide, because I'm really going to be dead talking about getting up on a witness stand. Don't you get that, bitch ass nigga, or is you just listening to the bullshit that's falling out of your ass?" he stressed.

I took time to take his scary ass remark into consideration, and at that point I could see all the gangsta shit this man had been pulling in the streets were in vain, because obviously Miami T and his son had put the fear of God inside this man. I knew of the reputation of the men, but actually seeing a man that caused terror in the streets, scared for his life, showed me things were more than real.

"Listen Baxter, I'm hearing everything you giving me, and my sympathy is on zero for right now, sir. This is only business, as you would say in your environment. Unfortunately, Capt. Williams doesn't give a flying goose's ass about anything these people can probably do, he wants your voice, and finger pointing out this man from a stand. We're gonna put his ass so far underground, every time one of his associates see you, they'll turn into fucking stone like Medusa was their reflection in the mirror.

"We won't let you die, Baxter, but we're definitely not gonna let you finesse us from the objective. Either you're gonna testify or you're gonna touch the streets in another ten years, after we take him and every other nasty criminal down around DeKalb County. It's your choice, but it can also be mine, Baxter. I'm trying to help you out here." I held my hands in the air, giving him my final and only warning.

His laugh sounded off, and it nearly looked as if he wanted to shed a few tears.

"You dirty, slime ass cops can't do nothing but bury me with this bullshit, and I'm not gonna be the only one losing behind this. You can bet your ass on that!"

"What the hell are you talking about?"

"Oh, you know, Brown. You think you can tell on a made man in this city and live? Please…it's inevitable for me, buddy. If I do what you ask, I'll either be a target from his people, the hood, or one of your crooked ass own. This is a game of the price is right, and everybody out there having enough to get whatever kind of business necessary, handled swiftly. So…if you want me to do it, walk in my cell and shoot me in the fucking head, and dissect the speech out of my brain, pussy. Fuck you!" He spit on the glass aggressively and stood, making his way out of the visiting room.

Leaning back in my chair, I sighed, thinking about the shit he just came from his mouth with. *Even one of my own?* It wasn't sitting clear, but I knew it was about to get critical if we couldn't get this fat scary bastard to sing.

Straightening the collar of my Hugo Boss collar shirt, I checked my watch, and decided to head back to the office to look up whatever I could find out about more close relatives to Miami T. It was gonna take somebody to break in order to see this fall, and what better way to try than a family member that's bitter for not receiving their cut, or portion of street fame. It was always the downfall of a rising star, and I was about to try my best to see it transpire.

Chapter 3

Mama Vee

Cabbage Town

I opened my eyes to the sound of a hard knock on Stacy's front door. T was lying next to me, and he was on the same accord with me, because he jumped out of the bed with me, grabbing ahold of his pistol. He pressed his back against the wall, looking at me with wide eyes.

"Who the fuck is that?"

"I don't know, genius, I just woke up beside you." I tossed on my house shoes, heading for the bedroom door.

Before I could even fully open it, Stacy was forcing her way inside with a finger over her lips.

"It's the fucking cops! T, you have to hide." She waved her hands around in a frantic pace.

This shit caused me to damn near panic. I grabbed my ass to make sure I still had it inside my body, 'cause I felt like I just pushed a brick out of my damn stomach, after hearing cops. T took off out of the room, disappearing to another section in Stacy's apartment, and my nervousness was causing me to shiver like a penguin. Throwing on a pair of pants, I made my way to the living room, and stood behind the wall, as Stacy opened the door for the authorities.

"Yes gentlemen, is there a problem, Officers?" She gazed out at the group of men in front of her door.

I could see a man with a white military buzz cut step forward, face ready to deliver whatever news he had printed on the paper in his hand. His expression said bullshit, but dealing with the police around Atlanta, you never could tell. I watched him flash his badge before he started talking.

"Good day, ma'am. Your name is?"

Stacy's face screwed up, but she answered, "Stacy Jones."

"Well, Ms. Stacy Jones, I'm not sure if you're aware, but your residence has been reported for harboring a fugitive. A fugitive that the department has on a mean shit list on the east side of Atlanta. You wouldn't happen to know who I'm talking about, would you? A man that goes by the name Miami T? Ring any bells?" he asked with his hands crossed.

A team of officers were armed, standing behind him silently, not including the load packed up around the streets. All I could pray was T found a safe place to hide.

"No, I'm afraid I don't."

"Well, that's just fine. I'm sure this search warrant will be sufficient enough to check while we're here." He handed her the paper and gestured for his men to head inside.

I froze up in the hallway when the men entered, not really knowing whether to run or lay down. Instead of making the wrong move, I just stayed still.

"Hey Captain, we have a female in the hallway." An officer pointed his gun at me with no emotion.

I held up my hands, watching the cheesy ass superior step in front of him, eyeing me with cheer.

"Wait, let me guess. Vee Carter, better known as Miami T's drag-along, or better words, half-wife. If it's not a surprise to see you here." He smirked, slapping me into a pair of cuffs, as his men continued to ram shack the apartment.

"Is there something I did wrong?"

"Well, besides laying up inside of this woman's home, that just gave me false information, by the way…you're the closest person to the man on my number-one wanted list in Atlanta. He's more of a prize possession right now to my department, and I might need your help locating him," he responded, leading me to the front porch to take a seat.

"I haven't seen my husband in years. If you haven't forgotten, you took him to jail the last time you saw me, Mr. Williams," I said with sarcasm running through my tone.

"Indeed, I did, but it should have been the both of you. It was my slip to ever think leaving you on the streets would stop the madness he was causing. Seems like the dirty work continued."

My mind was running on overload, and I locked eyes with Stacy, sitting in the back of police cruiser. Her lips mumbled something to me I couldn't make out.

"I want the entire home searched. Top and bottom, look through documents, clothes, any trail that'll tell us if he's been here."

His eyes rotated back down to me and for some reason, a cold chill ran over me. I knew for a fact that if T was caught up today, after hearing what I heard, he would probably never see the day of light again on the streets. Even worse, without me or his children. Smokey's face immediately dropped inside my mind. "Listen to me, Ms. Carter. I can see you've been through a lot. I've perfected my plans to make sure you don't have to go through a lot if you don't choose. These children, your life, your future...does any of that matter? Because if it doesn't, you can just tell me to go fuck myself. I'll ensure Child Services and a magistrate judge can get you proper visiting hours to see them for your assistance in false information, and party to a crime, for helping a fugitive remain on the run. It's your choice." He taunted me with his beady black eyes.

His all-black pea coat hung down like he was fucking *Blade*. He was just missing the blood sucking fangs that drained the life out of anybody making a slight income from the dirty game.

I stared deep into his eyes and gave him exactly what was on my mind.

33

"I'm quite sure you have the normal thinking process. You know, the kind where you try to break the average black man from his home. Toss him into a cage under a filthy prison where he can rot for life. Even throw all of the filthiest things on him, just to make yourself feel better. You're the bottom of the nastiest when it comes to a man that supposed to be a superior of the law. You are the line beneath the man of the house, looking to steal his position because of what you don't have. The one who's actually inspired by the heights the low man rises to without your dragging of schools, and ass kissing like how you fell in line. So…giving up my husband, even if I did know where he was, would never be through the hands of a muthafucka like you. So yes, Captain Williams, you can go and fuck yourself," I spat back to his evil spirited ass.

All I could get in reply was a demonic smirk and shrug. It was beyond my knowledge on what this man really had in motion for my man, but all of it was about to come to the light, sooner than later.

After listening to the police wreck Stacy's home for the next twenty minutes, they eventually came out with nothing, and all the rest of the theories I'd recently seen about the dumb pigs was shining clear as day. Captain Williams was the first to move back towards me, with a look of distraught. It was almost as if he wanted to choke me out because of his missing pieces. Pieces I would never place together for him.

"So, Ms. Carter, your friend will be going to jail today for false information and lying to a peace officer. Luckily, the weapons she has in her home are registered, because I would be slamming all of the little kiddies in a van for child neglect, and force them to whatever orphanage I could, before you had a chance to even get them back into your custody. I'll let you in on this little warning, Ms. Carter. Get out of Dodge and when you move forward, never look back because I'm gonna bury him, with or without you." He damn near grazed my ear-lobe with his lips from how low he was whispering.

Watching him walk off the porch, he turned to look at me, before jumping back into his unmarked 1991 Mercury. I watched Stacy nod to me, and that's when the feeling to grab the kids and get the hell out of that home, came over me. It was either two things. The captain wanted to crack a case for the glory, or he wanted blood for a payment that was far under the table.

Once the swerving police cruisers were out of the parking lot, I moved quickly back into the house.

"T? T?" I looked around the home, wondering where the hell he could have disappeared to.

A small noise and movement forced me to look at the bottom vent, connected to the bottom kitchen wall. Walking closer to it, the metal door fell open, and a hand slid out, scaring the shit out of me.

"T? How in the hell did you get in there?" I looked on as he crawled from underneath the water tank.

"You'll be surprised what I can do when it's time to get away from the police. What happened, where is Stacy?"

"T, they took her. She lied about you being here and they saw me, so they arrested her, feeling that she was hiding something. Her kids are here with our babies. What the hell are we supposed to do?" I nearly wanted to cry. Grabbing my face, he planted a kiss on my lips, and I could actually say his embrace calmed my energy. Even at the moment where something critical was occurring, his presence allowed me to know things were going to be okay.

"Vee, just get all the kids together, grab the money, and let's prepare to leave. Stacy's kids will have to come with us, until we can bond her out. Go now." He nodded towards the rooms where the children waited.

"Okay, okay. I'm on it." I rushed, doing exactly what I was instructed to.

Quickly getting all the little ones together, my oldest son Chris, eyed me with tiredness draining from his facial expression.

"Mama, do we have to keep running? Where is Smokey?" He caught me off guard with his question. I got down on one knee, rubbing his cheek with a light peck.

"No, baby boy, we aren't running from anything. But in order for me to ensure we are safe…I have to make sure I handle everything in my power, so you guys can relax and live free as you should. Until then, I will protect this family to the best of my abilities."

"Is Daddy and Smokey gonna go to prison?"

That question alone forced me to choke on my own words. I mean…it was literally same shit I preached to both of them daily, and now my child was stressing it as if he saw it unfolding to be true through his own eyes.

"No, Daddy and Smokey aren't going back to prison. We just have a few more things to handle, and we can put all of this stuff behind us, baby. That's all. Now get your things, and help the other little ones get dressed quickly." I kissed his forehead, heading back for the living room with T.

By the time I got back, he was on the line in a conversation with someone unknown. I didn't want to disrupt anything, so I stood to the side and listened.

"I don't give a fuck what he has to do. This crooked ass cop is back on my bumper, and I refuse to lose again, fucking with him. You have to trust me. Right now, it's something slimy going on, and I can feel it in the bottom of my gut. Stay out of the projects and keep a low profile. There's no telling who's after us. This shit with Chino is only the beginning."

I could feel the seriousness pouring from his words, and all I could do was silently pray God kept a shield over us until he sought us a way out.

"I love you too, man. Be safe," T said before hanging up, and turning to face me.

"Who was that?"

"Your son. I was just alerting him on my run-in with Captain Williams. It's not safe out there with this nasty ass cop running around on our trail."

"T, what the hell is the story on this cop, besides him arresting you back then, when he destroyed our family? Is it some type of mission to arrest our whole bloodline or something? I'm lost and I'm fucking scared."

Rubbing the small of my back, he placed a delicate kiss on my forehead. My nerves immediately began to calm.

"Vee, Williams is not the man he dresses to be. I have more dirt on him, that could swap the tables and send him to prison for life. Unfortunately, I'm not a snitch, but he knows what I know, which is why he's trying to find me. He doesn't want to lock me up, trust me."

"Well, if he doesn't want you locked up, what does he want, T?"

I kept pressing for the info I wanted to know, and I could see he was becoming frustrated.

"Listen, Vee, just know it's not my fault, but if we don't hurry up and get the fuck out of here, we ain't gotta worry about me going to jail, you will have to worry about the way you want me buried. I need you to trust me. Grab the money and kids. We have to go. I'm gonna take the back door and slide through the cut. Meet me at the gas station a few blocks down from there. We can talk about whatever we need too."

Instead of arguing and putting up a fuss. I contemplated on all my next moves to make sure I was able to hold on to my family. The remark about burying him was the final straw, and I was willing to go all out to make sure he remained by my side, and also our children's. Even if it meant my life being on the line.

Grabbing the money from under Stacy's bed, I moved back to get the children, and the rest was nothing to speak on. We were back on the road from Cabbagetown, until we felt the coast was clear for us to stop.

Chapter 4

Keith

Bowen Homes Projects

It was around ten in the morning when we finally pulled into the Bowen Homes Projects on the westside of Atlanta, for Smokey to handle his last piece of business before we hit the road. Not only was we riding around with two keys of coke, but we were clearly bucking against the signs of what my spirit was telling me. It wasn't the time to be doing hand-to-hand plays in the mix of so much trickery going on around us. We had too much weighing on a plate and not only that, but we were also still trying to shake back from the last major slip-up we had.

After Smokey parked, I grabbed the bag before we hopped out the car. I looked at this nigga getting out with his crutches as if he wasn't just shot less than forty-eight hours ago. He was more than persistent when it came to work. He was over professional. A precise maniac when it came to seeing this work get sold. It was like he didn't mind living on the damn edge, which always kept me bewildered like a muthafucka.

"Bro, didn't you just get a call from your dad, saying stay out of the projects? You're already on crutches, fool. We don't have to do this low budget ass work anymore, Smokey. You know this." I tried to reason with him.

"I know, Keith, but these are my folks. A deal like this will ensure us a lockdown on the west with the clientele, and that's what we're in need for. More people to shop. It won't be nothing but a few minutes."

He fed me the story he wanted, and I ran with it, but it was nothing like I saw it going down in my mind. Right after that, a woman came high stepping from around the corner, moving straight over to us.

"Smokey, Smokey!" She waved her hand, trying her best to be incognito.

I noticed her and patted Smokey on the shoulder to look behind us.

"Trinette?" He paused, stopping for her to catch up to us.

By the time she reached our personal space, a crowd of five men, stepped from around the same exact corner, except their smiles were upside down, and one happened to have a chrome 9mm Ruger clutched in his hand.

"Uh, Smokey, we might got a problem." I nodded my head to where the situation stood.

"If it ain't the man of the year. I thought you moved to the east side, this a long way from them sides ain't it, my nigga?"

"Damn Carlos, you still feel some type of way about that, huh? I'm not here to live, my guy. This your land, I'm just breezing through to see a couple of close ones. No pressure." Smokey raised up his hands in peace.

I couldn't do nothing but stand at his side, knowing that I just left the gun in the car, under the passenger seat. I cursed myself a thousand times in my head for not following my first mind, but I didn't want to stir up a panic at the moment.

"That's why I was trying to make it around here and tell you. Carlos is on the *Looney Tune* shit again." Trinette whispered, still facing our way.

"Well, you damn sho did a good job with that."

"Fuck that, the west side ain't doing no switching for nothing, but it's reasons behind everything. Word is, a nigga got a fifty-piece on yo head, and I wanted to know if you really did an act that can put you in such a shitty position?" Carlos asked with slanted eyes.

He wore a black hoodie over his head, and the leather jacket he wore had a few slits and zippers going around it like he was the hood Michael Jackson or some shit. I wanted to see how the fuck Smokey was about to clear us on this one, 'cause I was lost on what to do.

Look man, you holding ya sack bout some sucka shit. We could be eating and getting some money if you wasn't always holding on to that miscellaneous shit. And as far as me having anything on my head, a nigga ain't did nothing but pray on my downfall since the start of my movement, so what's new?" Smokey shot back.

"Smokey, reach for the gun tucked in my dress, grab it!" Trinette whispered.

"What?"

"I said, get the gun out of my skirt, it tucked in front of my stomach." She slid her hands out the way to give him complete access.

Smokey looked over at me, shrugging his shoulders. I wanted to deny him doing whatever the fuck was on his mind, but it was too late. Snatching the gun from Trinette's lower front., Smokey started to ride the clip, just as I shot off for the car sitting less than twenty feet from us.

"I understand, my nigga. For what it's worth, I take the blame for all the fuck shit that has occurred between us since we linked. You say fall back, so I'll let you steer and rotate this shit the best way you see fit. I'm with you, not against you." He held his fist out to me sincerely.

Returning the gesture, I nodded in approval, and thought about the real mission ahead of us. Making a three-day trip up north and back down, to have Rhestay his next payment in a timely fashion. Before it was all said and done, we were gonna be the ones with the small niggas eating out of our palms.

***

The next morning

Cincinnati, Ohio

Smokey

It was around two o clock in the morning when we took off on the road, with Pauline's brother leading the way. Not only did we have Janet trailing behind us with a food truck trailer, less than thirty feet at all times, but we were legitimate with the sheriff escort vans for the state of Cincinnati labeled on the side. I even had a few disguised inmates on board to ensure we made every trip perfectly, Coolio and Felipe. Not only did I trust them with me and Keith's lives, but I trusted them to handle the mission on terminating anything. Ty was driving one van, that held thirty keys, and I was behind the wheel of the next one with Keith, holding another thirty.

"Yo…Ty, I need you to bust a right on the next street and wait for me at the end of the street corner. This is the first clientele, and we've been driving for over ten hours. I wanna make this quick and smooth. They don't deal with too many unfamiliar faces, so me and Keith will take it from here. Once we're done, we exit the same way we came, with you taking the lead to push us towards New York." I spoke through the walkie talkies we recently purchased through the Radio Shack in Atlanta.

"Loud and clear, my man. I copy that," he responded.

Getting to the next street, he turned right and parked at the curb, turning on his hazard lights as me and Keith kept forward. Almost seven houses down, I pulled in front of the two-story home and parked.

Sighing, I looked over to Keith.

"I should be back in like five minutes. If I don't, come in shooting because this bitch obviously turned me into a catfish or something," I said, grabbing the supply of fifteen keys, laid neatly inside a brown Polo duffle.

"What the hell are you talking about?"

"Never mind." I put the strap around my neck and climbed out the front seat, using the walker.

I chewed on a few pain pills that had been helping me ease my nerves and suffering for the past few days, and they were working like a charm. It was crazy because not too long ago, I was just helping Keith around on his crutches, now I was the one moving like a cripple, not even a month later. It was really the reason I sucked in all the knowledge bruh was giving me the day before, after my little run-in with Carlos.

Stepping out, feeling the cool Ohio wind breeze against my skin, I headed up to the front porch of my destination. Two men occupied the yard, working on separate cars. I could tell that they were just advertising a fake ass commercial obviously, because both of them had holstered pistols on their hips. They eyed me recklessly, but neither approached, nor said anything to stop my movements, so I continued up the small set of stairs, until I was face-to-face with the front door. Before I could knock, it came open and my customer appeared out of nowhere.

"Hello, Smokey. I see you're an hour behind time like usual, Teddy gram. However, it's good to see you." Tisha Mae crossed her arms, looking at me up and down.

She was an older chick in her fifties, but magnificent enough to go for a twenty-five-year-old, judging from her toned body. Her hair was always in two goddess braids, and she barely wore make-up. She would kind of remind a person of Vivica Fox, with the attitude turned up a few notches. She was arrogant if I should say, but I loved the way she did business.

"Come on, Tisha, you know I'm not an office man. It wouldn't be right if I showed up with accurate timing on every deal, that's how you know I'm not perfect, but I'm damn sure reliable." I smiled shaking her hand delicately.

"Mmm-hmm, come on in." She stepped to the side, allowing me to enter the threshold.

The inside of her crib smelled like roses as usual, it was laced down with the touch of an old woman but as I said, the looks would fool you. I watched Tisha Mae's butt rock from side to side, as she walked in front of me for the kitchen. Her personal bodyguard posted by the door watched me with a nasty eye, forcing me to shake the ass from my vision. It was something I needed in order to make sure I stayed business headed, before my little head started to think for me.

Reaching the kitchen, I took the bag, sitting it on the table, and slowly pulled the kilos from the duffle. Tisha, took out a small razor blade, placing a tiny slit on top of one of the packages, sampling the new product we was dishing.

"Ooouuu shitt!" She shivered lightly and started to twerk in place.

The small little dance show was about to take my attention, until I snapped out of the hypnosis.

"Does that mean it's good, Tisha? I'm never sure when it comes to you."

"Of course, Teddy gram, because if it wasn't, I would've prayed for my priest to turn you into a caterpillar, before you made it back to Atlanta." She pointed a stern finger at me.

I wanted to laugh, from the recent statement I had just made to Keith before I got out the car, but I held it, keeping shit professional. Trisha moved over to her cabinets, reaching under the sink, pulling out a black briefcase. Prancing back over to me, she clicked the locks open simultaneously, rising to the top for me to view the neatly stacked hundred-dollar bills.

"Voila! All there, Mr. Teddy gram, of course you know the next time you stop by my house, you might as well leave the fabrics, in order to have a pleasant transaction." Her eyebrow raised with inquisitiveness.

"Huh?"

"Oh, let me be a little more clear. The next time you come to business with me, sir. I'll be requesting your pants to remain outside, and your dick to be informed on delivering some pleasure. Is that more understandable for you, black man? I don't speak out of feelings. I speak off authority, and it's about time to slide something different into our dealings, if you know what I mean." She bumped her hip lightly up against my private.

I nearly jumped out of my skin from the action, and her mean ass bodyguard was still looking like a human pitbull with mange, staring directly at us. Obviously, she didn't care or he didn't mean much, because she was more than forward with what she requested on my next visit.

"Uhh, I understand, Tisha. I'll try to make sure I leave the pants at home the next time. I hear ya loud and clear." I closed the case and prepared to head for the door.

She placed a hand on my chest, speaking one last piece before I departed, something that really gave me chills, regardless of her being high as a kite at the moment.

"Stay away from all islanders. You got beef heading yo way, baby, and my ancestors telling me you might need prayer, pussy, and pistols to keep you protected from the storm that's ahead."

"And which family member told you this?" I asked, starting to get a little spooked around this bitch.

Instead of answering, she led me to the door and excused me out with no more words said. Once the door closed behind me, I looked back for a second, and started to haul my ass to the car quickly as possible. I was from Atlanta, where statements like that only came about when a nigga was about to get played out of something. Or, robbed and smacked to the concrete from a bullet. I wasn't into feeling neither one, so I tossed all the lunatic antics clean out of my mind, and remembered we were on a time schedule to handle this business.

Jumping back in the transporting van, I tossed the briefcase into Keith's lap.

"Another one down and many more to go. Remind me to have you come deliver Tisha's supply next round." I buckled up and pulled off.

"Why you say that?"

"No reason," I lied, before turning to look back at Felipe and Coolio in the backseat.

"Next stop, New York, fellas. We gone swap labels on the van at a near garage to let you boys get a rest, and we back at it. Just remember, the bigger reward when we get back, is enough to buy whatever house you want on the north side of town," I stated before turning my eyes back to the road. Just as Keith said, leaving the bull out of the way with the small paper for the bigger bread, was gonna always win. I just wish I would have understood Tisha's words a little more clearly to know what was ahead of us.

Chapter 5

Manhattan, New York

Chan's Spa

Keith

It was nearly nighttime when we finally arrived up to New York. It was damn near a straight twenty-six hours of driving, and I was more than exhausted. Who could blame me if we were pushing over ninety something kilos all the way up north? I didn't need any wrong steps occurring with Smokey, so I was with him all the way, even though he was automatically a wrong stepper with certain situations. We were in Manhattan, the city of money, work and fame. If you wanted anything to sell, it was the right place to try and start. You could sell a mansion to the poorest muthafucka out here, so I knew exactly what some rich money could do.

Unfortunately, we weren't there for anything else but delivering our next shipment. I hated dealing with this Asian cocksucker. Not only because of his arrogance, but because of his remarks and boastful power. He wasn't the type of clientele I was intrigued on dealing with, but I obliged with the business, only because my dog was in the middle of the handling.

"Do I really have to get out the car for this one? I can't stand this cheese puff penis dork. He's a fucking bug." I rotated my head around the parking lot once we climbed out of the front seats.

"I mean, you want to keep the business all the way safe right, nigga. You gotta come. According to you, I might fuck around and kill everybody we supposed to be serving, or either they gonna kill me. You know your presence is needed. Plus, it's been going smooth like this." Smokey flashed me a bright smile, not caring about what I was feeling.

I had the twenty kilos of cocaine in my hands, as he led the way into the phony ass massage therapy parlor. For some reason, I felt like we needed Coolio and Felipe with us but carrying around a set of prisoners in the middle of the night, through New York City was surely gonna be beyond the obvious. So, we dropped them off at a local associate's home, until we decided to head to the next city.

Once we entered the building, a Chinese man in white scrubs, held a position by the door, as if I couldn't see the pistol bulging from underneath his shirt. It was definitely a nice setup because if you didn't know what you were running into, you were surely gonna die stepping recklessly through the establishment.

Smokey nodded in approval to the disguised bodyguard, heading to the counter, and rang the bell that sat at the edge of the counter. It was like magic, because Chan's boogie ass came from behind the silk covers, clapping his hands as if he was about to be served a five-star meal.

"Mr. Carter, Mr. Carter. I was starting to think me and you didn't share love anymore, my friend. I've been waiting for nearly a day. Junkies can't get themselves high, ya know." He broke into a fit of laughter, slapping his knees like he just said the funniest shit in the world.

Smokey tapped my shoulder as if I was supposed to coincide with the chuckles. I forced a smile and continued to remain quiet.

"I'm sorry, Chan. It's been a rocky trip, but we here, baby. You know, out of anyone, you would be the last I keep waiting for great business. Literally last." Smokey patted his chest with an apology.

"Good, because I would hate to be last, Mr. Carter. Hate." He squinted his eyes like he was trying to see if there was any flaw on what my dog was telling him.

I still bit my tongue, so I wouldn't speak on any of the slick talking. Just as I started to get frustrated, he motioned for us to follow to the back.

Moving through the fake ass velvet curtains, we walked past a couple of rooms being occupied with massages and ended up in a small gathering room where over ten gorgeous women sat around naked, chatting as if they were just waiting for the next fuck to come. Some were black, most Asian, even a few Puerto Ricans were in the bunch, and I had to say they did look magnificent.

"So, Mr. Carter, what do we have this time? Your last batch was quite the show-off for my customers. Had them falling out on the job. Me couldn't have allowed distractions while women being sold in my business, so I ordered no snorting at work." Chan took a seat in between two of the girls.

They both began to massage his shoulders and hands as he stared on. Smokey glanced over to me, reaching for the bag. Allowing it to fall off my arm, I handed it over. Taking a kilo from the bag, he passed it to Chan for testing. He handed the brick to one of the closest women to him, and she immediately slid a switch blade from her hip, puncturing the plastic for a sample. Watching her intently, she shivered from the raw cocaine, and gave him a satisfying nod.

"I see you have stepped it up on an old man. Do me a favor, try to ease down on the wigging drugs. Me can't have the women pass in and out on customers during a blowjob, right? They might munch down with their teeth and whoops, there goes your cock!" Chan burst into a fit of laughter.

I had to chuckle off that one, but looking at the time on my watch, I was ready to proceed with what needed to be handled—the money. Chan snapped his fingers, and a few women retreated to an office room behind them, returning with two small totes with our payment. They were dropped at our feet, and of course, I quickly bent down to make sure things looked proper. My eyes scanned the bills, quickly estimating what I could. After feeling secure enough, I stood back up, nodding to Smokey.

"Well Chan, it was good doing business with you, old man. You know as always it was a great pleasure. I'm only a phone call away, so I'll be waiting on your next ring for our future meeting." Smokey shot the deuces.

"Uhh, wait just one moment, fat man. We're missing something." Chan crossed his leg with anger etched on his face.

"Excuse me, what do you mean?" Smokey scratched the side of his head in confusion.

"Your friend here. It's his first time in Chan's spa. I don't know if you're up to date with the tradition in my place of business, but when someone steps in here, we don't leave without happy endings. It's security procedure, plus a habit of my establishment."

"What? Smokey, what the fuck is this jerk-off talking about?"

I knew I wasn't tripping, so I was positive what my ears were taking in was more than accurate.

"You heard me clear. No one leaves this place without me knowing whether you're wearing a wire in business. Unless you're scared to get a blowjob in front of these beautiful girls that fuck for a living. Clothes off," Chan said as more of an order this time.

"Look Keith, it's just the way he operates. Let's just get this shit over with, so we can get back on the road."

"What type of freak show is going on around this mutha-fucka?"

"The type only millionaires get to experience. I'll see you fellas in about fifteen minutes, top." Chan tossed up two fingers in the air and headed inside his office.

"I think this might be my last time traveling as a drug trafficker. Might as well invest in whorehouses, and porn films," I said, unbuttoning my shit.

"Welcome to the big league," Smokey replied before we were dissected by the women in front of us.

***

Zone 6 Precinct

Detective Murray Brown

11:48 pm

I had been on my bullshit, investigating the new treachery taking place now around my area, since Miami T and his shit-head ass son, Smokey Carter appeared out of nowhere. My crime rate was rising by the second, and every other hour the department received a new call about a fiend, overdosing on the new drugs that had just slapped Atlanta into a frenzy. I was furious, pissed beyond diapers to be exact.

I forced myself to work a few extra hours to take a look into the savage-minded animals I was dealing with, to make sure I came correct when the time was presented. I knew they weren't amateurs from the nine-hundred-thousand-dollar bust we'd just gotten a whiff of a few months back. It seemed like since the names came up around the department, a lot of silence arose, so I started to do my own digging.

"Hey Brown, I'm leaving, I'll be back around six for the board meeting. You should try and get some rest." Officer Williams stuck his head in my office, with a look of exhaustion.

"Loud and clear. Hey Williams, let me ask you something?" I stopped him in his tracks.

"Sure thing, sir."

"The drug board we're observing right now…these guys we're chasing…tell me your input. If the drug rise has been up ten percent since six months ago, what would be the first conclusion that pops up in your head for the outlet?"

"An out-of-country connection."

"Exactly, and what places do you know delivered such a drug that zombified the entire city within less than a month?"

"Well, Cuba has the most potent cocaine, besides Colombia, but the access of getting the drugs back to the states are beyond slim. So, in order to move the product, it would have to be somewhere closer, much closer to slip pass the law without being seen. That would be Florida or the Bahamas."

I pointed a finger at him to show his thought process was making some fire sizzle in my mind. It was smart to stay down south with the product movement to keep a low profile, it was the reason the loss in Orlando was nothing, which meant the plug had to be closer than I thought.

"What's the drug causing the overdoses we've been hearing about for the past week? Cocaine. What's the easiest way to grab cocaine from down south without being seen? A car, which means our drug lord has to be straight out of the closest thing to the water, the Bahamas. Williams, I need you to search the top drug peddlers out of Miami and the islands in the past year, because one of those men is obviously gonna be our man." I snapped my fingers.

"I'm on it, sir." He rushed out of my office with a new-found energy.

Quickly pulling up Miami T's case, I snatched the records and started to look a little deeper in the mix for the accomplices, or defendants involved around him. The information I located shocked me, from what my eyes scanned across. It had to be my blessing from God himself.

Frederick Watson, aka Fresno. Deceased 1975-1990 born: S.E. Florida, Bahamas.

Chapter 6

Smokey

Essex, New Jersey

Jareo Owens Car Dealership

I was more tired than a bitch who'd been fucking out both pants legs, and we were just now reaching the last drop off to my clientele out in Jersey. Pauline met up with us at the bridge to make a swap with the trucks, and head back down south with Felipe to recover the funds from all the trap houses we had going. I didn't want me and Keith's presence being gone with the wind for a few days to cause niggas to start getting bright ideas. Shit was smooth, and that's exactly how I needed to keep it. Ty was a new edition to the team, and his magic with the transportation was magnificent for our process. We were literally moving stars, and sliding straight past the pigs, rocking out.

Ty pulled the van inside the car dealership's parking lot and parked backwards inside a space. Keith lifted his head, as if he couldn't believe we made it.

"Finally! You guys should be able to knock this out with a piece of cake, so I can go lay-up with my woman after this. I'm trying to be back through the city limits by morning. Let's breeze this." He leaned his head back against the seat.

I laughed, tapping Ty's shoulder.

"Aye, grab the bag and walk with me, Ty, let's allow lover boy to rest them pretty ass eyes, while we rake in more of this cookie batter. Let me know if you would rather work the spots now. Me and Ty could look nice doing this shit." I laughed, climbing out the front seat.

Ty followed me across the lot of exotics. It was beautiful. So many collectors and old schools. Cars you didn't usually see in the streets of a Georgia area, unless you were on the outskirts. I knew when my check got to where it needed to be, three, maybe even five of the best cars would probably be parked in my lot. It was all to come in the middle, when I stepped up to where I needed to be in the game.

Walking through the glass doors, we stopped at the counter, where I spotted his usual secretary. The blonde-haired white girl, that popped bubble gum like she never ran out of flavor. You never knew what type of weird ass folks you would meet, but I wasn't discriminating when it came to making bread. I would learn later it was my downfall.

"Hey sweetheart, can you tell Jareo I'm here? Tell 'em I ain't having that much time." I tapped on my watch for emphasis.

I was hungry as fuck, and the fake ass security outfit was itching to come up off me. It gave me chills just wearing this fuck ass shit. As I waited patiently, Jareo eventually strolled from the back with his head down, talking loud as a muthafucka.

"Is it my man? I mean, my main man!"

He was speed walking, and finally lifted his head to greet me, when his eyes landed on me. Then froze in place as if he was being stuck up. He stared back and forth between me and Ty like the thought had been knocked out his head.

"Uhh...Jareo, you okay, my guy?" I waved my hand in the air curiously.

He snapped out of the trance, and immediately got on some real crazy shit. "My bad, my friend, how can I help you? I was just pondering to myself for a minute and got lost." He shook my hand lightly.

I eyed him weirdly, wondering did he just have a sprit fly in his ass, cause his posture was most definitely different.

"Was sup is these bricks you ordered, Spanish, fly ass nigga. I drove way up here, what the hell you mean, how can you help me? You couldn't have forgot I was on my way?" I laughed as if he was shooting a joke.

"Excuse me? Bricks? I have no clue what you're talking about, sir. This is a car dealership. We sell cars." His face was straight, uncut from all games.

"What? Jareo, you need to cut the games foreal now. Let's handle this. I need the money so we can be back on the road." I tried to ignore the fake act he was putting up.

"Sir, I'm beyond serious. I'm afraid I will have to ask you to leave, or the authorities will be contacted. I won't ask again." He held up a finger towards his assistant as if he would give her the approval.

My ears couldn't believe what the fuck I was hearing, and I had to look back at Ty, looking just as stupid as me. Once I faced him again, and he still pointed towards the entrance, I knew it was surely something fishy in the air. I wasted no time backpedaling out the door, getting back to the vans.

"Yoo Keith, get the fuck up," I yelled as we jumped back in the van.

"What?"

Cranking the engine, I sped off and didn't mention another word, until we found the expressway heading back south.

"Jareo just flipped the script on us. He didn't buy the work, and just started acting crazy out of nowhere. The muthafucka threatened to call the cops when I said something about the supply. It was something wrong."

"What? Hold up, Jareo spends more money than anyone of my uncle's clientele, are you sure you were speaking to the right man?" He rubbed his temple in confusion.

"Man, that's the only Spanish, pony-tail muthafucka in the car dealership with an accent. Of course, I had the right man."

"Oh, shit! Did he say anything about Blue?"

"Uhh nah, unless you mean calling the blue suits on me, fuck no!" I sweated, gazing in the rearview.

"I gotta tell my uncle, it's no telling what's that's gonna create. We never had anything out of the ordinary happen with this guy before. It damn sure didn't just figure to start today." He reached for his phone.

"Wait, you might wanna wait to do that in person."

Taking my advice, he held his composure to deliver the news. Not to mention, we had Ty in the car, and he didn't need to know more than he already did at the time. Using my reasoning, I placed every possible thought in my head, on why the Spanish mark flipped on me. I was clueless. I knew one thing for sure. I wasn't stopping the van until we were back in the safety of our home. I wasn't about to slip up on the road with thirty-plus kilos. Wiping that shit from my mind, I started to accelerate on the gas.

***

Keith

Blue's Crib

Opening my eyes from Smokey tapping my shoulder numerous times, I looked around at my uncle's driveway and exhaled. It was more than a blessing to be back. It was time for a few days towards a break, because the dope money was starting to become a headache as usual when the flow was pushing fast. It came with pros and cons, but it was a job I had to mentally build myself to perfect. It was just the way I moved when I needed to concentrate on new strategies on per-fecting us, my uncle's foundation. At the end of the day, it was me too, but it would be nothing without him.

"Bout damn time, where did you drop the logo man off at?"

"In front of Pauline's. He jumped in his own shit and said he had more business to attend to, so I thought we would head over here to see what he had to say about the shit that hap-pened in Jersey," Smokey replied.

"Well, that's something I'm dying to know." I chuckled, stepping out the car with my right hand behind me.

Coolio was still quiet, the same way he had been the entire trip. I knew my uncle kept him around for a reason, and han-dling issues was definitely one. I didn't feel like our lives were in jeopardy from the stunt Jareo pulled, but I did feel like he was playing some treachery somewhere in the fields.

Using the key to step into my uncle's home, the first per-son we saw standing in the middle corridor was Felipe, posted up on the wall, along with three of my uncle's killers. I knew it was a problem because we only kept one bodyguard around at a time. The house was quiet, and nobody said a word when we entered, not even Felipe.

Strolling past them into the living room quarter, I stiffened up from Blue holding a black 9mm handgun to Pauline's head. She was tied down in a chair, face battered from whatever struck her face, her eye was swollen horribly. My mind flew totally left bound, wondering what the hell was going on.

"Blue, what's going on?" Smokey and I stood side by side, waiting for him to speak.

He nodded at his bodyguards, and they moved hastily to the wall, standing post. His full three-piece suit was fitted to perfection, and he was dressed as if a meeting was about to start with the commissioner of the state. Clearing his throat, he gazed down at Pauline.

"Well, nephew, it seems we have another problem you two have caused. A serious problem that has officially ruined my name, and the layout of my business. When I sent you two on the road, it was for you to find the best way to deliver these drugs to the clientele the best way you two could. You two." He smiled, masking his anger.

"Ok…wait, what happened? And why do you have a gun to Pauline's head?"

"Let me ask you something, Keith. Where is the guy supposedly named Ty?'

I paused for a moment before giving my reply. "Smokey dropped him off at Pauline's spot. He rode with us to do the drops and came straight back, no flaws. Why?"

"Well, nephew. I got a call from one of my closest friends, Jareo, from Jersey. We've been friends for a very long time. I mean, business so good you could leave a key in the center of his street block, and it'll still be there days later. He said you guys showed up to do the usual dropoff, but this time was different for him, you should say," he spoke calmly.

"Unc, I'm confused, because Jareo pulled a stunt when we showed up. He never bought the package, plus he threatened to call the cops, that's what we were showing up to tell you."

"Yeah Blue, he flipped a dime quick."

Blue laughed to himself, before striking Pauline hard across the head one hard time. *Whack!*

Blood squirted from her head as she groaned in pain, falling semi-unconscious.

"Well nephew, thanks to you taking this bitch right here with you, it helped me figure it out. I caught her talking to the so-called brother on a call after she arrived back, speaking about you two being suspicious of his movements. Like a ghost that appeared out of nowhere, right? Seemed funny because I thought she had true intentions to bring good people around to actually assist with our family business. That was until the next call came to my phone from Jareo.

"He said when you entered his dealership, he came to solidify the business, and he happened to see a person he never could forget. A person that helped testify and lock his brother away in a penitentiary four years ago. I know you aren't the man he was speaking on, so it came to my attention that you two took an undercover on a full tour of our fucking sales. Ty is a fucking cop, and this bitch fed you dumb asses right to him!" Blue delivered another hard slap with his backhand.

"What the fuck? No way, I knew it! I fucking knew it." Smokey slapped his hands together back and forth.

I was so distraught because he tried to warn me about the phony. Even the look in his eyes was shaky. On the road, he remained quiet until he was spoken to. He paid attention to everything we did, every move we made, and every stop we took. He was investigating us, and we gave him an entire book. The thought of him taking flight right when we got back to the states said enough. It was no telling where he was doing or planning against us to pause our survival. I lowered my head in failure.

"It's my fault. I can't believe I allowed this to happen. What do you want me to do?" I asked with a straight face.

Complaining was the bitch way out, and I was ready to accept my admonishment right then and there. It was a part of the game, and right now a fed case was probably being built against us at that exact moment.

"First of all, I want everything switched up immediately. Cut off all clientele this Ty guy has seen. Find him, and do him the worse way, no empathy. Before any actions are taken from this day on, alert me before you move. From now on, I tell you who to serve, who to let in, and how to proceed. Get new customers in the bounds of the state. Pay Rhestay and build the foundation big enough to where you can handle it, before you lose it. Plus, she's all yours since the work was devised by her." He tilted his head, holding the pistol out to me.

I stared at it for a second feeling my stomach curl. I hadn't done the dirty deed in a while, and it was something I tried to rarely bring out my closet. But when disloyalty crossed the bounds of our home, we had no choice but to protect it with all honor.

Smokey looked back and forth between us, wondering what was next, what had to be done. Pauline was slumped over in the chair, barely moving from the beating. I stared at her in disgust. Grabbing the gun from Blue's hand, I placed two quick shots into the side of her head.

Boc! Boc!

I listened to her gasp for air, chest deflating, releasing gas from her body. Blood started to run profusely down her head and face, before I placed the gun on the glass table, taking a seat. Smokey's eyes were wide in shock, but he didn't speak a word about what just occurred before his sight.

Blue swallowed the shot of tequila he had in his glass cup and huffed lightly.

"I'm disappointed in you, Keith. I trained you all these years to watch you slip when an extra face comes around. I'll tell you this. If this guy right here in front of me does no justice to our lives and business, handle him the same way before he destroy us. But if he's worth it to you, teach him, and make his ways come out immediately. I expect to see you both in the morning," he said before walking off into his home, leaving us alone.

I looked up at Smokey's angry face and expected to hear the bullshit come out next. Instead, he said the complete opposite.

"I understand his reasoning. I have no fight against it. I understand if you don't want me around anymore. I'll just sit back until you get at me with how you want to handle this fucking cop. You can find me at the Westin." He sighed, heading for the door.

When he exited my uncle's home, I crossed my hands, placing everything that was really eating at my skin across the table, and I honestly knew what we had to do next. It was time to become an animal with the same people that claimed to be predators. It was the only way to allow our voices to match the opposition's. My kind mask was off and I was prepared to get dirty for the win.

Chapter 7

Tracy

Cabbagetown

A couple days later, I was released from the county jail, on bail for the charges I recently caught at my home. It was too slimy for me to rat out T after all the loyalty he had shown, it was owed more than anything. Even though I nearly took a fall with losing my children, and on the verge of being killed by some complete strangers, I was standing harder than a tin can under my grandmother's fridge.

Sneaking out to my home in the early hours unnoticed, I used my key to slide through the front door, quickly closing it behind me. I shook off the light chill from the small wind that chased in behind me. I had to get to the savings in my safe, and get a few valuables to change locations, the first thing that crossed my mind when I started walking towards my room.

The tall man that jumped from my hallway nearly made me tumble and fall backwards, but my hand didn't hesitate to grab the .357 I'd just stopped and borrowed from a good friend of mine. I let off three shots, hitting him in the stomach and face.

Boc! Boc! Boc!

But the vicious kick that blindsided me, forced all that to end. The gun flopped out of my hands, and I nearly pissed myself from the blow, as my brain shook hastily. A man grabbed me by my hair, snatching me from the floor.

"Agghhh!"

"Look at this little bitch right here, y'all. We got us a tomb raider on our hands, don't we?"

My vision could see another group of men with guns, surfacing from around the corner, stepping over the clown I just wasted.

"I'm glad I just hired that guy this morning. That means I would've had to kill you quicker." He laughed in my ear.

Before the room grew silent, there were five armed men in my living room, and a man choking me like a pitbull dog. I fell to the floor, gasping for air, when he released me. Looking up into his face, he smiled like The Joker.

"First, I'm gonna introduce myself, and if you play wrong, on my dead brother, I'm gonna shoot you in the fucking head. My name is Chino," he spoke and reached for the zipper on his pants. Pulling out his dick, he put it directly in my face.

"First, you're gonna suck my dick to pay me respect for my dead soldier. Open your fucking mouth." He pressed the barrel of the gun against my forehead aggressively.

I nearly cried, shivering from his tone. I knew his mind was far from joking, and I opened my mouth, cringing from his index finger twitching lightly on the trigger. Within seconds he was jamming his manhood into my mouth, gripping the back of my head.

"Do it!" He pressed the gun down harder.

Bobbing my head lightly, I took him in, closing my eyes from the embarrassment. He was pumping like my shit was a vagina, and I nearly puked on the floor, but continued to do what I was told.

"That's what I'm talking about," he grunted as saliva started to run from my mouth and nose. I felt his piece rise and release into my mouth, forcing me to jerk away and throw up everything in my stomach.

"Woowwww! You the mean one, girl. That was the introduction of Chino, and you handled yourself well."

He fixed himself and took a seat on my sofa directly behind him. The pistol was still clutched in his hands, tapping lightly against his leg. He was staring, he wanted something that I couldn't guess, and his stare only made my mind run into the wall with an answer for why.

"Listen, I'm gonna be straight forward with you. I drove way out here from Alabama to come and handle some specific business, and I didn't come with intentions on wasting time. Now usually, I would save myself time and just kill anyone I find until I get the person I need, but I guess God is telling me to try and be fair. You can look in my face and clearly see I'm not a fair man, baby. Neither are those men behind you. So, this is what we'll do." He came closer and kneeled down by me on the floor.

"You're gonna tell me exactly where Miami T is, and everybody he loves. I must have this information because it's the only way I can proceed out of this shithole. So, are you gonna let me know, or do we gotta do this the hard way?"

I tried to calm my chest from heaving in fear, I could feel death creeping up my spine. Crossing out the people dear to me was a way I never could portray. My lips moved to speak, but I couldn't.

"I'm gonna give you one more chance to speak up before I leave yo head under the carpet. Where is these niggas? Please don't try and be a hero, lady. Save yourself." He wiggled the gun around to scare me a little more.

Remaining firm on what I believed in, I tightened my pride, and bit my tongue to stand for what I wanted.

"Fuck you, sucker. Do what's best for ya." I wiped the tear from my left eye.

I refused to let him see me sweat before whatever happened to me that he was planning from the start. Watching him stand back to his feet, he removed his jacket. "It looks like we gone be here for a minute guys," he huffed, looking down at me.

***

Simone

College Park, GA

It had been a few days since I had heard from the mystery man that I was definitely feeling a little too hard. It never failed. I always ran across a handsome man that was involved with something I never had room to be a part of. Just my luck, this one was one I actually got involved with quicker than I thought. Watching the big screen television in my living room, I laid in a pair of blue Chanel shorts, and a fitted Gap T shirt. A pair of sky-blue footies rested on my feet, allowing me to soak up the heel-free time while I was resting. I was so used to being on the move and staying busy, I barely had time to even consider what I wanted to do with my life.

I was already through college, with my master's degree in business and management. I was credentialed, down to work or associate myself with whatever enterprise I chose. Instead of using my face card, I decided to go in search of creating my own business and become my own brand. Now, running into this thug had ruptured my brain for the hundredth time, even though I wanted to kick him out of my head like an evicted resident.

A firm knock at my door forced my thoughts to be placed on pause. I didn't want to move my lazy self off the couch, but I managed to drag my emotions up to my feet and answer it anyway. I opened the door without caring to ask who it was. When my eyes landed on Smokey, I just knew the Lord had to be playing miracles with me, because I didn't just predict this nigga up to my porch. I quickly rubbed a hand through my smooth curly hair, forcing a smile.

"Well, hi. I mean…where did you just appear from? I was actually just thinking about you," I stumbled with my words, crossing my arms nervously.

He was smelling like Prada cologne, and his shave and cut was on point. He wore a black Polo shirt with matching loafers. The bleached Burberry jeans he wore gave it a more casual look, making him even more attractive and date ready.

"Well actually, I was just in the area and remembered you told me to stop by when I got the chance." He gazed at me with his pupils scanning me gently. I could feel his eyes piercing my skin like he was physically touching my body. This guy really had a spell on me.

"So, you just happened to be in College Park this early in the am, it must be my lucky day. Especially not knowing I would actually see your face again. You're like a hope and curse at the same time," I said truthfully.

"Damn, hope and curse, what does that mean?" He leaned up on his one crutch all smooth, with a questioning face.

"It means you could be a woman's hope. Someone that actually gives a girl good faith, something to look for when its nothing else to want or search for. But becomes a curse because it's never any telling if you will actually be able to succeed with applying that, with your ties that pull you far away from being that gentle person. It doesn't mean you're a bad guy, just a bad chooser with decisions."

"Maybe you can teach me a little about that, since you know about that area." He brushed a portion of my hair back from my eyes.

My stomach felt as if it bubbled with a pot of butterflies drifting around my belly, and it was on my mental to hug this good smelling man to calm my interest down a few notches.

"Do you mind if I come in and sit with you for a while?" he asked me, catching me off guard.

"I was just about to slip into my nightgown, boy. "You really caught me down bad being lazy." I waved him off.

"Maybe I can help with that. The whole lazy thing."

"I don't know now, Mr. Some of these drama movies can get really interesting. You ever seen *Thin Line Between Love & Hate*?"

"I have. Still, these movies can't interact with you how I can." He slid a little closer to me.

I felt myself weaken and my thighs started to tremble from his intoxicating cologne. He was absolutely a king in my eyes, even an addiction. All I know is I felt comfortable with him around. I really couldn't help it.

"What will it take for a man like you to hang the streets up, and call it quits for good? Is it money you're after? Women? Or maybe that answer is too knee deep for you to answer. In the end, is the visit worth it? More than living a life where you don't have to look behind your back? I studied him as he evaluated my words. He rubbed a hand through his head, which let me know he was putting together whatever he was preparing to say.

"To be honest, Simone, there is no such thing as a good life when it comes to living, protecting and working for what you want, need and got. I do what I do because I don't want to see my family have to struggle, trying to make it in this free world. Not every family is blessed with a soul that will get out there and hustle by any means. I put a business suit on in my mind when I walk into the streets, because that's all it is, business. If I was to drop everything right now, and say I was willing to run off with you, wherever around this world. Do you think we gonna survive off finances, or us just hoping things will be okay? If you don't work, you don't eat and that's just the way it's always been on this cruel planet."

I shook my head, thumping him across the head with my finger.

"Boy, it's no such value on life, and waking up another day just to see the people you claim to love. I would rather have that, than to have any money at all. It's only materialism ruling, a way to handle, a way to control. As long as people continue to treat money like it's worth the world, instead of a piece of paper. We will always have people that feel like they need to go get it. That's honesty, Smokey." I fed him a piece of my mind.

He was rubbing my cheekbone with a smile, and before I knew it, he was leaning in kissing my lips softly. I thought my heart almost stopped, but I was sure I was still breathing. I applied the same pressure, kissing him back, and once our lips broke apart, I stared in space for a few seconds. Obviously, he felt similar to my bewilderment, because he was rubbing his goatee as if it was about to fall off.

"Can I tell you something, Simone, I mean speaking from the heart, not my feelings?"

"Sure."

"Are you sure you can listen to me open-mindedly, and respect how the heart feels?" he asked before continuing.

"Of course, I wouldn't want it any other way."

"In this world, I've only adapted to one thing in life, and that was making my own way. I've never had the chance to feel empathy or compassion for when I needed something or wanted anything. It was always a place that left me in charge at the end. I'm involved in a dirty lifestyle. One that consists of me trafficking drugs and doing things half the men out here dream of accomplishing. I've never been proud of it, but at the end of the day, I stand on what I do proudly, because I handle what I have to in order to remain first. When I step in the streets, I put on a business suit, because that's just what it is, business and nothing more.

"I can't neglect what I'm used to and just to be real, even if I had a chance to leave the game right now and hang it all up, I would crush those chances under a car motor and let it suffocate, because it will never happen. I can say this. I've never felt the emotion of another person having love, care or any thought on my well-being, so maybe that can actually start to give me some kind of influence with what I would like to become. I would like to have you. I want you. But I also understand if you don't want to deal with me, because of my dealings. It's respect."

He sat back, rubbing both of his hands like he was waiting for a trivia answer, and I had to really salute the truth he just gave me upfront. No man would lie about what they felt, because it would show in his actions. He was straightforward, and that alone let me know he had enough respect to at least be truthful with his mind and soul.

"Smokey Carter, I have to say you are a stubborn man, but I also have to admit you are cold with the way you rock your attitude. I like it. I may not support the drug game status, but I damn sure support a man that would like to put in an effort."

We shared another quick kiss, and it was unfolding in front of me that I actually might have a keeper in front of me. He would have to receive some crucial criticism, which I didn't mind doing whenever I felt it was needed, but he was a man I could work with. "So, I'm guessing that second kiss was you locking me in as your girl, huh?"

"Actually, that was solidified on the first kiss, I just had to make sure I secure you for the second one." He blushed.

"Whatever boy. Let me find out, cause I won't play to fight yo ass. You a real one and I can see that, but you ain't gotta be nobody else with me but Smokey Carter. Not the richest man in the game, or the hardest, just Smokey," I stressed sincerely.

He nodded never taking his eyes from mine, and that was a true bonding moment for my little heart. I was really around the presence of a gold one, and I was going to keep him.

"Let me find out you stalked me down to tell me everything I want to hear."

"That depends on if you accepted what I just said. I've had my eye on you, but I wouldn't stalk you, it'll be better if I just pulled up to ask you for your hand in relations." He chuckled.

I giggled like an elementary school girl meeting her first love. It started off as a shitty day, but turned bright for me, as this man walked into my inner space. I was just hoping that I could keep all the rest of the non-sense at bay, so we could really lock in for the ride. I was down for it however it came.

Leaning back in for a sneaky kiss, I was surprised to feel him wrap his arms around the back of my neck, sucking my bottom lip for dear life. I embraced it all in one motion and before I knew it, I was slipping out of my shirt. Fire wasn't the word I felt crawling around my flesh, it was an inferno. He removed his shirt right behind me, and the next thing I know, I was in the mix of some shit that bitches didn't get a chance to brag about if they were smart. The temperature was high, and I didn't want it to end once it was ignited.

Chris Green

Chapter 8

It was early the next morning when I woke up to Keith's phone call about meeting up at Blue's. It had been a disaster for the last few situations, and it seemed like they were only getting worse. My input could only stretch so far, especially with me standing behind the man, to receive any position at the table. It was part of the game. I took the punches as they came, but I wasn't the type to tolerate failure to much. If I was gonna be a partnership at my man's business, then I was in for the long run. It was never the hand to bite, when you were saved, and fed. That's what my dad T stressed more than anything. Loyalty.

Jumping inside my rental all-black Excursion. I headed over to the location and cleared the trip within less than thirty minutes. It excited my blood to be handling real business, but now that I was really in, I saw how easy a nigga could fade to the black and slip.

Pulling into Blue's driveway, I parked the large truck beside his original 1998 Corvette. I shook my head, thinking about Pauline, and how easy it was to be around the plotter if you were careful. It only showed me no one was off limits.

Knocking on the front door, I was granted access from one of the house guards and moved straight for the living room. Keith, Blue, and another individual I wasn't familiar with, occupied the sofa's engaged in conversation.

"It's about time. I was starting to think you retired on me already." Keith walked over to greet me with a handshake.

"Please. How can I leave you, when you didn't leave me. You're my brother, crazy man."

"Those are factual statements."

Blue's eyes studied me for a second before nodding, gesturing me to take a seat.

Of course, I didn't reject. Finding a space on the couch next to Keith, we fell into a small moment of silence, before Blue cleared his throat.

"Smokey, I want you to know when we deal with problems, we keep those problems between this family and table. Understood?" He stared at me deep in the pupils.

"Crystal."

"Good. Now me and my nephew, we eventually talked after our little pandemonium, or whatnot. It happens. What type of life is it, if it can't be shitty some fucking days. That's just the reality part of the truth. I ceased all old clientele and linked you all in with new buyers. That means no extra people. No discussing. No slips. Disassociate yourself with anybody is of yesterday spending money with us. It's just a charge with the game.

"I've hired extra men at the new spots we have running, and it's up to you two on who's gonna manage that. Regardless of who, make sure it's no one you have love for. Because if the time comes, you will be the one pulling the trigger. We have money to make, and also money to pay. Rhestay is getting a little aggravated, and it's starting to bother me. You have enough to set up the next pick-up, so pay him, and begin a fresh week, to make this process speed up. I can't afford to lose this plug, neither can I afford to hear any more disappointments."

"Oh, I can promise you, the room for mistakes is excluded from our vocabulary. The next crooked turn, and bodies will turn along with it, right then and there. We're gonna tighten this shit up, that's just what we do." Keith shrugged with confidence.

"Indeed." Blue inhaled on his cigar. "And I've been Superman since they replaced me with the Clark guy imposter.

It's always room for slips. Just make sure we're not the ones tripping."

"So, what should we do now, all of the connects are on pause, we can't afford to sit around and wait for the petty money to cash in from the houses. It'll take forever to accumulate the last two payments for Rhestay. We gotta move, but how?" I asked to be sure we were all clear.

"All you have to do is relax and press for what we need. The hood is filled with money, it's just in other fools' pockets. How do you get that money out of their pockets into yours?" he asked.

I couldn't say off the top of my head, so he answered for me.

"You force them to. Anyone that's serving around the city, force them to join us. We have better product, more avenues, and guarantee loyalty. If they refuse, make them agree. Once the agenda of everybody running for our team hits the wave, we will have people paying just for us to be merciful and not crushing their entire necks. We have the men, and we have the respect. That's final."

I nodded, damn sure liking the sound of what the old man was kicking. It was time to boss it up on the real mafia level. It was either join or stop. It was foolproof, and if we applied pressure on all the serious heads, Atlanta would be in our palms.

"So, do we just go around killing any guy that refuses? We might as well get a little bail money to the side." Keith learned forward looking between both of us.

"No, nephew. Kill the heads, and the bodies fall. Only whoever's necessary and oppose a potential threat. Execute immediately and regroup to building and earning. "We aren't accepting no, not even from the friends of ours," Blue said with no emotions, and puffed on the cigar harder.

"Cool, maybe this opens some answers on why close ones have been dropping around us. We still got our little visitors in town, so this is the perfect time, to call the bluff. I'll be collecting from all the spots today and establishing new rules. The ones that don't accept neglect."

I listened to Keith speak and couldn't do anything but respect the mastermind that he and Blue unified to devise. Now it was just time to show up and execute.

I noticed we would probably have this moment to discuss this. I'm excited. I haven't been around a good mission in forever." The man on the opposite couch spoke for the first time.

"Oh shit, I nearly forgot, Smokey. This is my little brother, Echo. One of the most solid shooters and best nerve-wrecking muthafuckas you'll probably ever meet. He's the most special thing I got left in my right pocket, so sometimes he has to disappear when his head unscrews from his body but meaning well is what he's built from. Echo, this is Smokey, my right-hand, and business partner that's gonna help me rearrange this damn city." Keith introduced me.

Leaning over to shake his hand, he grinned from ear to ear.

"It's always a pleasure to meet anyone rocking with my family. Keith is a hate bug, so if you was able to squeeze under this sack of shit, you're damn near family. The feeling is mutual if my brother trusts you, my man," he added.

His light blue eyes were definitely dark as death, and I could tell by his strong energy he had done a few things that would scare the average weenie in the streets. He was an evil spirit in the flesh, and his vibe was clicking with me off top.

"The pleasure all mine. I'm used to being under Keith and scurrying around the battlefield. I fit right in." I laughed sitting back, easing my tension.

Blue smiled but stood to his feet, pacing slowly over to the large, double-curtained window. His hands crossed behind his back, and I could see from the look of his face that he was having one of those domination thoughts.

"All I want is excellence. I want it all, and I've never wanted it all. Make an example out of everybody. I want a stain so dirty that it carries our name for the next forty years. We are the elites. Now go tell them." He tilted his head towards the sunny street.

Echo jumped up first, and Keith followed right behind him. Standing up, I glanced at Blue and nodded silently. What was understood didn't have to be explained. If he wanted the city, it belonged to him. The thought of what Simone told me yesterday crept inside my mental knocking like the heavy hand of a cop with a warrant. It was like déjà vu. I knew the wisdom she gave was the perfect, simple-made truth. It was truly just hard to accept walking away from what I was best at. I wasn't just the average Joe, the rookie dealer that tossed the truce flag in the air for help. I was Smokey Carter, the real plug of lil Mexico.

***

Janet

Cobb County

After finding out the news about Pauline, I couldn't do anything but shed a light tear, and kick her snake ass to the back of my mind. Smokey called me, breaking down the recap on what the slick bitch tried to run down, until Blue sniffed her out. I had been out of work for days, and all movement for my customers had mysteriously come to a stop. Deciding to take my stash and relocate, I stopped by the house to pick up the last few keys, I had stashed in the floorboard. I wasn't going to warn anybody but Blue on my new location so the product will be strictly confidential.

Creeping through my back door, I gathered all my shit like clothes, important documents, and drugs in one pile. It wasn't hard to pile it all inside two individual tote buckets. Once I felt I had everything that placed a trace of me around the home, I snapped the lids on the containers and slid them to the door.

Booooom!

"Get the fuck down! Down! Down!" I watched a SWAT suited man, speed through the front threshold. He was toting a nasty gun that looked like it would shoot without hitting the trigger. Not only that, at least ten more was falling in directly behind him. Before I knew it, I was being wrestled to the ground and slapped in a pair of cuffs, before an utterance could escape my lips.

"Living room secured." The SWAT member radioed, with his hands restraining me on the ground.

The rest were roaming and shuffling through the rest of the house. Once it was searched quickly, they all gathered back in the living room. One of the dick heads wasted no time opening the containers and finding the few bricks I just packed. It was no doubt in my mind I was gonna receive a twenty to the door, just from my past history.

The feet of a suited man stepped into the house, and all attention flew in his direction. He was scanning the home like he knew every inch, and the year it was built. His eyes landed on the officer holding the kilos and smiled like a gremlin.

"Looks like we caught our cat. Now, the only question is where is the mouse?" he asked, a rhetorical question in the air.

He moved swiftly over to me, eyes downcast like he was God, looking over his creations. I didn't blink nor speak, but my eyes and curled lips said all I had on my mind.

"Well, Ms. Whoever The Fuck You Are, I congratulate you on standing up in these big ass shoes that obviously aren't yours. It shows women still can play a part in the deceiving ass criminal world. It was the reason I had no compassion, even when they beg. It's a grown world, and we make the decisions we want.

"I guess you got it all figured out, can you take me to fucking jail now? Save the sob ass story for your grandchildren, pussy!" I spat, knowing my journey was far from over anyway.

He laughed, clapping his hands lightly. He was the exact replica of a snake, and you could hear the hiss in between every word that left his tongue. The smell of some shiesty shit was going on, and I couldn't put my finger directly on the source. I made sure I watched intently, every move they made, even the words. It was gonna be the only way I slid my way out of the cracks, if my lawyer spotted one tiny flaw.

"Only a dumb bitch would speak something so reckless and stupid. Are you on your cycle and just furious? You wouldn't happen to know where Miami T, or his son Smokey Carter is at right now, would you?" He folded the wrist buttons from his pea coat back.

"Of course, I do. They're up your ass on the far right, and down south on the hill in your fucking small ball sack. You can find them right there on the corner." I snickered, toying with his mind.

"Shuttt the fuccck upppp!" He kicked me in the center of my chin.

Chapter 9

Coolio

Walking out of the gas station on the four-way in East Atlanta, I walked slowly over to the gas pump, placing it inside the slot to fill up my tank. My hands were occupied with a Brisk lemonade, and a pack of Newport shorts, that I was trying to pop open right then and there. It was the day I had to place a little disappearing act on my agenda, in order to ensure the heart of Blue's table continued to pump fiercely. I hated what I did, but I was comfortable with handling the business. Killing was like breathing to me, and the only time I found a small form of peace was after I expunged another soul from the earth. It was my job, the only job, Blue, and Smokey paid me well to do. I had to plot out my next hit strategically, because it was clear from the call that missing wasn't an option.

My head was so distorted in my own thoughts, that I never recognized the three Lincoln sedans cruise smoothly into the parking lot, stopping less than twenty-five feet away from me. My heart and adrenaline started to rise, and that was the sign that forced me to raise my head. My eyes landed on Chino, moving towards me with three more men, all toting guns raising to aim at me. Without hesitation, I stumbled back, snatching the River P8 from my waist, releasing shots at the same time as them.

Bloom! Bloom! Bloom! Bloom!

Poc! Poc! Poc! Bak! Bak! Bak! Bloc! Their guns matched mine, as if they were on the same rhythm.

I shot one nigga in the chest, watching him fall and before I could catch my balance, I felt a slug enter my shoulder, knocking me to the concrete. I still didn't stop hitting, as I jumped back on my toes like a cat, taking cover behind a bright green Ford truck.

Boc! *Boc*! *Boc*! "You dead, fuck nigga. It's all out, fool," I heard Chino yell through the gunshots.

My arm instantly went numb from the bullet, and I had to use my other hand to keep my strap busting for my life. Blood was dancing on the ground with every inch I moved but dying wasn't on my list for today. I was breathing harshly, leaning over the side of the truck, popping two more bullets from my gun.

Bloom! *Bloom*! *Bloom*!

Boc!

Another shot found its way in my chest, and the speed of everything switched to slow motion. I felt my breathing fall like a quarter from a skyscraper, forcing me to fall on the ground. I clutched my gun, trying to catch whatever wind I could, as I watched the fuck ass nigga walk down on me with his goons. Cars were swerving left and right to get out of Dodge, and I felt like the sky was turning gray from the blurriness forming in my eyes. It was fucked up. I lost and was caught slipping when I never screwed up. I was actually watching my life flash before my eyes, and I tightened my muscles, trying to lift the gun when Chino's face popped over me in my line of vision. The barrel of his gun raised up to my forehead, and a breeze forced the hairs on my neck to stand up.

"I'm gonna murder every last one of y'all niggas. It's no hiding!" he said through clenched jaws before I watched a bullet fire from his chamber, causing darkness to swallow my vision.

***

Mama Vee

Abbeville, GA

1:30 pm

It was hot and humiliating, in the middle of nowhere, and I was nearly about to crack a nerve if I didn't receive some closure on all the fuckery I was being put through. Ever since my husband came home, and mixed paths with my son. I found myself, fighting for me, and my children's lives more as the days passed. Not only were we innocent, but it was all for a past beef I've always spoken against since the beginning of time. I was sitting in the country with my babies, including all of Tracy's children. I still had yet to tell those kids their mother wasn't going to be showing up to get them, and part of me felt guilty.

It was all over the news how they found her body inside of the apartment brutally raped beaten and executed from three gunshots. I nearly wanted to jump off a bridge, thinking about the way this lady lost her life, for the sake of a man that didn't give a flying shit about laying back from the fire. T was pressing more problems on us to find out what was going on, but he only ended up with a bucket of confusion, and another charge laying in the wind to catch back up with him. We were being compressed by his behavior, and he didn't see the effect it was having on our family.

Watching his car pull back into the dirt road driveway, he hoped out with a bag in his hand, heading inside. Right when entered the house, his sight landed on me, staring at nothing but the wall. My face showed no life, no form of happiness. He sighed with exhaustion as if it pissed him off without asking a word. It was perfect, because my energy was beyond fucking mutual.

"Vee, what's the matter?"

He sat down in front of me calmly like nothing was more important than his ego. He showed no emotion for our losses, and the aura from his spirit made me want to walk away from the backyard hideout, with my children beside me.

"Well, I don't know, T. I guess life, maybe death. Maybe we been ducking fucking bullets ever since you stepped foot out of that damn jail. It's like I can't even close my eyes, because there is no telling when a killer might break in to murder my fucking kids, me or you. I'm sick of the ditches. I'm tired of falling over, and over, and I'm ready for it to end. Now." I rotated my head his way so he could look at the disgust slide off my expression.

"And I'm guessing you got the plan on how we're going to accomplish that, huh Vee? You musta went to sleep envisioning that I coordinated the hits on our seeds purposely before I slid out the slammer, just to see you in pain. Go ahead and point your finger at me to say I'm the murderer, cause I'ma be the fucking blame regardless of what peace I speak."

"You don't feel like you're part of this blame, because you can damn sure ask me that question again and again, but there will be no switching my answer. I fault you for the dealings. The love for the game that poisoned your mind to feel it never had an end. This shit is from your past, and it's creeping around us from the dead, because you still dance with the skeletons that created them.

"You're my husband, T. The same man I entrusted in. The one I gave everything up for, even my career, to raise your kids, because I was the so-called woman you adored greatly. Well, I guess those promises were left void, and after all my good deeds, the streets slept with you more than I ever could. Is this life? Hiding out in the woods, secluded from the world for God knows how long!" I cried.

"So, what the hell do you expect me to do? I've tried to hunt these fuckers down and handle it the old-fashioned way, but it's not gonna blossom overnight. You feel like it's easy to just say walk away. That'll be me just agreeing to a bullet in the back of my head, if I want this to end, if we want our family to be safe. I will have to keep my head on eliminating every bitch that had involvement on sending harm our way. It's nothing that can be let go, Vee."

I stood from the chair, shaking my head at his stupid ass remark. I couldn't believe I was literally talking to the same man that placed a ring on my finger.

"T, have you ever thought of just packing us all up, and just leave, never looking back? We have the entire world to use as our home, and we remain in the trenches of where we are most vulnerable. We can just start over, have you thought about that? You don't have to chase these fools around, because not too long after, they would be getting rid of each other for a different cause beyond yours. We could be Ghost's to these people. Why can't we, T?" I held my arms in the air, explaining my view on the bullshit.

He huffed with anger in his seat, rocking like he was the correct guidance regardless of the speech I preached. The devil was getting to him horribly and it was sad to say, but I saw him losing his life in the belly of the beast. All because of pride, revenge, and pain he couldn't bottle up and allow to let fly. I felt it every time he spoke. I was dropping tears as he choked on his next comment to bark against me. It was suicide at its best, and he was throwing my entire family in the blender along with him.

"Vee, this is deeper than you know. It was never my intention to see you or our children cry. I never wanted you to experience harm, and I felt I could do with getting what I need in order to feed you all. It's all I know, and I never intended the entire bridge to fall on us after I agreed to walk away." He lowered his head. I wanted to hug him to show my sympathy, but I wanted to slap the hell out of his ass to see if he still had any more life left in his dumb ass heart. It was coming down hard on our family and I hated to be the one to say it was his fault, but it was. My options were getting slim as a model, and it left me no choice, but to start making some decisions for myself. Walking over in front of him, I made sure what I was about to say was clear and straight to the point. Either we were gonna start deciding on shit as a family, or I was gonna take my kids and walk out the door to my own life.

"T, I can't do this shit anymore. This drama. The saga of never-ending bullets and blood. I'm done with it. We've been together since our teenage years, and I don't want to see us rip apart because you feeling like fucking *He-Man* out here in this world. You either end this shit immediately, or I'm taking the kids and walking. The decision is up to you. You have two weeks, and I'm ready to move out the stat. Either we're gonna leave together, or I'll be building my own somewhere out where it's none of yo damn business. Choose wisely, T. I love you. The kids love you. And we can't remake this family." I spoke my peace and walked off, leaving him to himself.

We were beyond the quicksand, and I was watching my man drown. It was critical when you could possibly die trying to love someone, but still die without having a care for emotions, period. I was ready to push off and leave Atlanta behind me, no matter who was with it.

Chapter 10

Smokey

Polo's carwash

After getting the info about Coolio a few hours back, my head still couldn't shake the sight of what the fuck took place. I already knew who was behind it, but the thought of our best hitta getting taken down like that looked awful on our behalf. We were stacking shit up on the plate by the load, and it was still rising. Blue was struck by the news but didn't hesitate to make us keep the plan in effect. There was no pulling back, and Coolio's blood was definitely the bell ringer that was about to be set in the streets.

Watching Keith finish chopping things up with Polo about his property, I roamed the area with my eyes, pondering on this shit with a heavy scale. I was ready to activate, and it was embedded in my heart. Just as Keith was walking back towards me, my visual locked in on the identical Lincoln sedans pulling into the store across the street. It was like Felipe recognized the same thing, because we both started to stare with the gaze of a hawk.

It was like my heart stopped when I spotted Chino stepping out the car. A few dudes got out behind him and it was like my soul stepped outside of me for a minute I know that me and this nigga had to be feeling the same way, because his eyes raised up and looked directly at me. Before he could even give me a reaction, I was pulling the pistol from my hip. Felipe was right on beat with me, whipping out his piece. Our guns sounded off at one motion, and the chaos began.

I fired six clean shots, and I was sure Felipe was probably at four, that's how quick shit swapped on us.

Bloc! Bloc! Bloc! Bloc! Bloc! Bloc!
Pak! Pak! Pak! Pak!
The roar of gunfire erupted, forcing him and his clown ass soldiers to take cover. We traded fire back and forth, as me and Felipe ducked being the wall of the car wash booth. Keith ducked his way through the fire and made it behind the safety of the wall like a jet. Within seconds, it was a full-blown shootout in the middle of Kirkwood, and it was not lacking.

I let my gun pop three more times.

Bloc! Bloc! Bloc!

"Fuck," I snapped, realizing how quick we just ended up in more tar.

"Smokey, we gotta get the fuck out of here. You can't shoot it out with these asses on main street! It's to many witnesses.

Felipe still rocked the clip out with his pistol, and Chino's mean was still answering back.

Boc! Boc!

Two ricocheted bullets bounced off the car wash's wall, ringing my ears. Coolio's life was on my head so bad, I still didn't want to move from my spot until I watched that pussy die. However, I knew what Keith was saying made plenty of sense until we had more of an advantage.

"Smokey, let's fucking go," he yelled at me, quickly starting up the car.

"Fuck! Let's go, Felipe!" I snatched him by the sleeve of his shirt to the car.

You could still hear gunfire sounding off as we jumped inside, skating backwards out of the parking lot. If our luck couldn't get any worse Dekalb County police came around the corners like a pair of phantoms, lights blaring and swerving to block off the street.

"Damn it!" Keith hit the steering wheel, heated.

"Fuck that! Go!" I aimed my pistol at the cruisers letting go a few rounds to stall them off.

Bloc! Bloc! Bloc!

Felipe even shot at them bitches. Keith mashed on the gas and sure enough, we came straight up out that parking lot, swerving past the pigs like NASCAR drivers. The few officers that had stepped out of their cars were trading bullets with Chino's team, and it was perfect for us to slide right off the scene with ease.

Make a right!" I shouted as we came up to the next street. A few back corners later, we were heading on the expressway, making our way across town. It was a miracle we had just escaped the fumes of Chino and the folks. I could damn near see the end playing out in my face, but it didn't go as I thought.

"We gotta put word out about this, nigga. He needs to die, and we can't waste any more time. Put a check on his head until we can lay on this bitch and smoke him out. He just murdered Coolio, and we run into the nigga not even three hours later? He's too close for comfort."

"I agree. I'll make a few calls, and we need to execute the business quicker than planned today. We have to do this correctly." Keith stood with my reasoning on what was just said.

He was doing a ninety on the dash, and we were flying like bats out of hell to spread ourselves from the scene, and what we had to complete by the evening. It was war. The tricks were falling out, and it was officially an all-out war. If Chino thought his ass was swiveling around the city like a wild bottom feeder, looking for life. I was about to end it for him.

"We can make a stop over here on the west side and pick up a few men, and more guns. We need some answers, and I'm not taking no for an answer. This nigga here stupid, and we're not about to sit here and wait for them to keep chasing us like prey. I'ma handle it easily. I'll fill you in later." I cut the conversation.

"Respect had to be earned, and we've had it since the beginning," I voiced, going back into my thoughts again.

The rest of the ride was silent. The level that was just lifted another foot had everyone trigger-happy. I made a quick stop over in Collier Heights to a local friend that helped me plug in with getting guns whenever I needed them, any kind. He handled his business out in the resident apartment but was living right over on the east side not too far from us.

Parking the car, we all got out, and headed down to Building 36. Taking a deep breath, I knocked three times on the bright red door. It took a second, but after a mumble or two on the other side of the door, it opened after a few latches were unlocked.

"Smokey? Damn fool, you look like you been in a fight. Everything good?" Retro smiled.

Stepping inside, I allowed Felipe and Keith to relax, and spoke to my handyman.

"We need guns. Good shit. We in a lil jam and it's getting real out there. Like now. You know I don't mind paying." I pulled out a roll of hundreds and slapped them in his palm.

He stared at the cash for a second and glanced over my shoulder at Felipe and Keith. It was obviously written on our postures. He didn't think to question me on why. Instead, he tucked the money in his pocket, and waved me over to the kitchen. I didn't speak, just followed. When my eyes landed on the table and counters laced with all types of artillery, I took a quick second to take in everything my eyes viewed. There were handguns, Rugers, Glocks .380's and even a few assault rifles. My sight caught the black pistol-grip pump. Resting against the wall, it looked like a fresh roll of duct tape had just been wrapped around the handle. Of course, I wasted no time throwing it across my shoulder.

"I need boxes of bullets. Give me two of those Glocks, two of the Rugers, you can give me one of the .380's too. I don't need nothing that's been used," I stressed that off top.

"Nothing in my place has been used, Smokey. New serial numbers, new metal out the box. You know how my merchandise come." He started grabbing everything I requested.

I watched him box it up for me, and instantly started to load the clips, right in my exact spot. If we were gonna do the real thing, I wasn't about to play. I was gonna murder every nigga I possibly could, to show them exactly how we were coming every time.

"If anybody ask you, we were never here."

Retro assured me with a nod, but his twitching hands made me think twice in case the word happened to come out. I grabbed the guns, being sure to hand Keith and Felipe a gun each. If we ran back into trouble of any kind, the issue would be handled on sight.

"We gotta make one more stop, before we start cleaning up the issues. If we get this side to stress Blue's weight, we'd lock down the exact territory to run that shit up like air balloons, my nigga. Until then, we all in." I looked at both of my closest companions at that present moment. I was officially the reaper now, and I was ready to prove it.

***

Bixby Court

Making the last trip over to one of the most dangerous apartments on the east side of Atlanta, the mission was simple. Slide out there, letting our faces be known. Holla at Roosta, a known grinder from the city. Firm and direct, and never went without showing love back to the hood. It was just my luck when I approached with the propositions to shop with Blue for the best, and we all pushed money through the same circle, to make sure it comes back around. We chopped it up for bout a half-hour before I left. We had a new alliance trapping the same stamp we were pushing. I knew it was only so much more in play for us to grab and bring on the winning side. We had to move steady with all the friction setting off. In order to be ahead, we had to stay moving.

Looking at my watch, I realized it was time for us to meet Rhestay for the drop off. It was another three meetings, and it was all gonna be over with. We decided to meet at Ms. Ann Burger spot, on the east side. It sounded a little confusing when it happened, but the small joint for burgers was the spot he picked. It was weird, because we were on our side of town. Not only did we have Chino creeping on the low, but we were the underdogs, which meant we could get hurt anywhere. It was the reason I wasn't going to let my guard down.

"Is there any reason this guy picked the east side to do a pickup for two hundred fifty grand? I would think he would at least want to keep our business a little more discreet."

"Yeah, I was thinking the same thing. I mean, I know the nigga ain't tryna rob himself, so he's the least of my worries. Delivering the money successfully without any dysfunctions is the main thing I'm running across my mind. Those thoughts stayed on my mental until we arrived at Ms Ann's restaurant. The crowd was light, and nothing seemed out of the ordinary besides the all-white Rolls Royce, parked sideways, filling two spaces. It was clear he arrived before we did.

Getting out of the car, Keith frowned, but he had a reason to. A quarter-million was in the book bag he was toting, and the time for asking questions could come later. The sun was baking me down, but the quicker we handled the business, the better. It didn't take us long at all to make our way inside and get to the table where island man sat enjoying a dressed-up burger. He was accompanied by three of his killers, and their heads were moving around like a camera with sensors. They all had a head full of rastas, and a nasty mug was engraved in all of their faces.

"Smokey, Keith! Me was starting to think you boys have lost all the ethics to proper business. You could never pay to be late in my part where I rest my head. We take that to the heart. I'm always at business, an hour early to make sure I can't be late," Rhestay stated calmly, before biting another time out of his sandwich.

Nobody was eating in the building at the time, besides a few guests that were minding their own. It was always a form of disrespect coming from the islander vibe each time it came to dealing with the debt. It's almost as if he's daring us to get angry or stand against whatever he devises from his lips. Keith didn't speak, neither did Felipe, and their faces said the exact thing that was on his mind. They didn't want to fucking be here.

"Yeah man, things kinda got messy for us today, and we ended up getting caught into some shit that we couldn't just turn away from. Still in all we handled it, and still came prepared with the exact amount of what we agreed on, like last time. It's all there." I reached for the bag Keith had in his hand.

Taking it, I placed it on the table, scooting it generously over to him. His bitch ass safeguards were clutching, and looking greasy on the strength, and I was definitely not getting a business partner vibe from their side at all. It was like silent, hidden tension somewhere, but I couldn't tell if I was accurate or not. Keeping my thoughts to myself. I waited until he finished chewing and listened to what he had to say.

"Black man, where I came up, excuses never broke the chain of consequences when an agreement had been placed on the table. I built my legacy, mind, and lifestyle off that principle, and I wouldn't break it, not even for me." He pointed a finger sturdily at me.

"You sound like somebody I know." I nodded with respect. "But to be honest, Rhestay. We do what we can, and if the best doesn't occur, then we try it over. We're not robots, not God. We're only hustlers. Ones that always pull the best results when it come doing our part. That alone deserves some respect, don't you think?" I asked to see if the cold-hearted bastard could accept some truth.

He chuckled, holding up his hands. I guess that indicated whatever I said meant nothing, in his eyes.

"Smokey, I've been in this life for a little longer than you've been born. I mean it when I say I've lived the best and tasted the worse on days where I didn't want to. It was my spirit. My name. When a person asks me, they will rather not speak, because of how serious I carry me self. You try, is what a small child would cry and say. Men, businessmen, complete the job.

"We don't half-step. We stomp and continue to stomp until your heart explodes from being consistent. That's the agreement we have, mon. I don't allow weakness around my circle, and I would have the first person killed that goes against me when I voice it. You two are great business, and that's the only reason I deal with Blue for supply. After this debt is cleared, another fall like this will place us at opposite sides of the table where I eat from, young one." He imitated a gun firing to his temple.

Keith's eyes lowered with hate, and I saw the tricks Rhestay had up his sleeve, and I wasn't buying it. My mind was catching all the slick shit, and I was steps ahead of what my counter would be. There was no flaws in my plan, and I didn't intend on allowing one to creep in.

"Rhestay, I respect you sir, truly. And business will continue like usual, while I try my best to tighten the strings on whatever you feel is placing a default in our paths. Excellence should be expected all the way around, so I can't do anything but salute your wisdom, and keep it close to heart where I can't forget about the mistakes it caused me. It's accepted, big man. You have the floor, so we breathe off your advice. Is it safe to say same time, next week. I'll allow you to choose the location," I stated humbly, feeding him on.

Slowly nodding at me, he whispered something in Patois to his closest henchmen, and laughed.

"I like you, Smokey. keep that thinking and heart, and you will roll over anything you come up against. That is, with me behind you." He cheesed, holding out his hand for a shake.

I wanted to haul off in his ass with a barrel of hooks, but inside feelings were gonna remain inside when it came to winning this fucking chess game. It was no fun when the rabbit had the gun, and I was starting to feel like Bugs.

"Indeed, Bossman. We'll be waiting on your call, and all will be set, as always. Guaranteed." I shook his hand firmly, never inching towards a smile.

Turning around to Keith and Felipe, I tilted my head for them to follow me out. Once we departed from the building, I spoke once we reached the car. Jumping in the front seat, I waited until the boys jumped in, and pulled smoothly off.

"Buddy is the main enemy we need to watch out for. It's something on his chest, and I can feel it every time we come face-to-face. The laws of business were simple, and it was never supposed to come with emotions or intentions. That was when the ill will started to fall from a person's smile, exposing their true mask.

"What do you mean? You think Rhestay is plotting against us?" Keith looked confused and lost on my statement.

"I'm saying his energy is bigger than the aura of a damn spirit, haunting the person that murdered them. It no way to hide it, and I call the shit out every time. It's like he's actually mad we're handling the business with knocking down the debt. He wants us to be slaves for him, even Blue. It's all in his words when he speaks," I replied back, glancing in the rear view.

"Do you want me to handle it, big bro?" Felipe asked with a straight face.

"In due time, lil bro. Right now, we only playing defense, and when it's time to strike, I'm gonna allow you to move how you please for that blood."

He took my response in with silence, and I already knew he was ready to get active on the turf. It was the only way we were gonna survive and destroy whatever we have on our plate.

"So, what are you saying? Should we find a new connect, and tell Blue to ditch this muthafucka? Cause I'm not trying to play duck-duck goose with invisible people that want me dead. I'm starting not to know who in the fuck at our throats. If we lose Rhestay and his reach across that water, we lose damn near our entire operation. I mean, this is the way it's been going for the past nine years since I was a child. He's a little rough around the edges, but no one can touch the type of supply he can, uncut. He's using the strings with that shit heavy."

I thought about how stupid he would feel when I switched all that up, because if the customers aren't happy, the barrier starts to fall.

"I'm two steps ahead of you, Keith. All you have to do is watch how the rest of the movie play out for us," I assured.

Being that I was creeping through the traffic where I was just having a full bullet fight in the streets, I made my way to the small clinic out in Kirkwood we called Baby Grady. They were known for treating niggas that got burned or catch the pack for fucking with them nasty ass fiends. I wasn't coming for none of the above, but a woman was definitely on my brain. The woman that could save me from whatever if she put her two cents, and ego into it. She was one of the best hustlers I'd ever seen, ever since I was a jit. If I had to handpick somebody to run a spot for me with no flaws, she would be my first.

Once I entered the facility, I roamed the room with my eyes, and searched for my long-time friend. After running past her three times, I locked in on Marcy, posted at a table, signing some papers as if she was built to secretary someone's office. It didn't even fit her image. She still looked the same. All her hair was still in, and she hadn't lost an ounce of her figure. The old cougar was something serious when looking through a grown man's eyes. Her aura could attract anybody, and that was the reason I was linking up with her again, to build something that was too solid to break down.

Strolling over to her desk, after a teenager jumped his young ass up from the chair, I calmly took a seat and smiled. Her head was still locked in on the paper, and she didn't even realize I was sitting directly in front of her. Her eyes eventually raised, and she nearly leaped out of her seat, wrapping around my neck like a choker.

"Smokkeeyyy! Oh, my Goddd, boy. You look good. Where the hell you been?" She slapped my arm playfully.

A couple of co-workers stared in our direction, and she didn't hesitate to wave them off with a hard hand.

"Fuck them. I haven't seen you since you were a baby bug, nigga. How the hell did you find me like that?" She grinned ear to ear.

"Well, first of all, I trucked through all of the old spots you used to be at and came up short. You know I'm everywhere, mama. I ended up running into one of my personal shooters over here in the hood, and he broke the water on you working right down the street. I had to come pull up and lay eyes on you personally. You still looking good." I rubbed a hand across her soft backside, laughing out loud.

"Smokey, you crazy. Seriously, it's good to see you, and I'm glad you sincerely checking up on me. But I know you way better than you think. What did you really come here for?" She stared into my face, waiting for a reply.

I didn't want to just bring the issue out upon her at the exact moment, with all the shit she had going on. It was hard to keep great eyes on something we were barely around to keep record of. That was the purpose for Marcy, with her iron fist, to jump back on board with me.

"It's nothing, Marcy. I—"

"Yo ass better not lie to me either. Spill that shit." She examined me to see if I might throw another fast one out there.

Shrugging the procrastination from my system. I kept it straightforward.

"Look, Marcy. Me and my main guy Keith have a nice movement going, and when I say nice, I mean beautiful. I've escalated with the game since the last time you were in front of me, but it's sad to say after all the help you instilled in me, I still had to make a way to turn and come back. I need a person that can run a main stash house for me. Sort of like management, to keep eyes on the funds and product, without any fumbles. Shit so ugly out here, it's hard to trust anyone, and all the falls we've taken was scars to the body, because it's not occurring any more on my watch. It's the reason why I thought about you when this agenda crossed my mind. You get whatever you need, and I'm paying top notch to make sure it's strictly smiles on your face while you're there. This is the part where I need you to show up for old-time's sake. You still my suga mama or what?" I said, smoothly rubbing a hand gently through the side of her hair.

"What the hell have you gotten into, Smokey?" She smirked with a low gaze.

"Like I said. The time for your help is needed, and if anybody can fix this, it's you."

I had to talk smooth, and sensitively even though I truly did it for the sake of the business. I couldn't let the bridge crumble while we were still crossing, and it didn't matter what it took. I gave Marcy that begging baby "please" face. She turned up her nose in aggravation, but when she stomped that damn foot, I knew we were in the game.

"Shit boy, you still can get on my nerves after all this time. Just please don't start complaining."

"That's the Marcy I know. You sound like you love the young Smokey again. Are you ready?"

"Now, Smokey? I'm at work."

"Fuck this job, you never needed this anyway." I held out my hand to her.

She stood still for a second as if she was nervous but obliged. People in the establishment watched us as we walked towards the entrance without a care in the world. Not only did I have the plan to get back on top, but I had the necessary keys with me to open all the doors.

Chapter 11

Detective Brown

Bright and early of the following morning, I was walking into the office to go search up some more information about Miami T's family, and just so happens, the captain was in the middle of a meeting. Instead of me proceeding off on my own mission, I sat down and tuned in to what was heading our way.

"I have one officer dead, and two men critically injured at the hospital for a shootout that we have no suspects attached too yet. In a better sense, I would say that whoever is responsible for this needs to burn in a furnace. It just so happens... we live in a world where things do not work like that. I'll say this one time and one time only. We need to find these guys and erase them off the streets. Either they surrender, or forcefully bury these sons of a bitches under whatever prison possible. We can't let people that have shootouts with the authorities remain on the streets I'm telling y'all now, we have a small window to make this happen. If we have no further questions, everybody is dismissed," he said while staring at us all.

I remained in my position, and he eventually locked eyes with me. He was an off-balance man when it came to showing emotions, which is the reason he never lacked on the job and position he was given. He pushed smoothly over my way, until we were face-to-face.

"Sir, I know it's been a rough forty-eight hours for the department, but I think this guy Miami T is more than responsible for the actions that's been going on. He's the star of the fucking streets right now."

"I thought I told you to focus, and leave all the thinking to me, Brown. This isn't the time for you to be playing cops and robbers. It's serious. Either you stick to your job description, or you know might not have a job to come back to, if the wrong action is made." He looked at me with a serious expression that forced me to think twice.

Still in all, I knew the capabilities I had of progressing with the case. If I took the renegades away from the streets, anything else would only be a small target to clean up for the mayor's happiness. How could we actually say the streets needed to be cleaned, but never got to the same criminals that's causing the treachery.

"So, what the hell should I do while all this is transpiring. Go buy a fucking coffee at Starbucks?"

"You should, but after around about nine o'clock. I want you to go and check out a place over on the east side, The Rib Shack. It's supposed to be a known hangout spot for all the high-ended criminals that surface this bottom-feeding ass neighborhood. If you happen to find a man there by the name of Lil Reggie, rumor tells me he's a worker for Miami T. Maybe he'll come off a little more info, instead of you running around chasing a bunch of ghosts. You have to start from the bottom.

"Start from the bottom? Sir, we're detectives, we never have to start from the bottom. Is this training school or something?"

"It wouldn't matter what you think it is, it's about the rules and steps you take to make the bust, not a failed attempt. You do it my way and you get results, any other way and you're gonna lose."

I took in his words, but I never chose to keep barking up the tree that was already on fire. He was persistent about leaving Miami T and his dirty-hand son in the wind. It was the only thing confusing me. We had killers and dealers on the loose, hounding out all of our model citizens. Agonizing the residents with their slaughter of malice murders, and crack slanging. It was the epitome of a true devil. I just couldn't do anything to cease it, with the captain on my back.

"Yes sir, I'll be sure to go check it out."

Turning around to leave the precinct, it was like I could feel his eyes burning a hole through my back.

"Brown?" He called my name out loud. I turned around to see him still standing in the same spot I left him in. "That's an order. Don't be late, and don't stick your badge into nothing extra. Just check the place out, and report back." His words dragged out with emphasis.

I nodded in compliance and headed out into the streets on my own mission. A mission that would probably make me lose it all, before I had a chance to take any one of these bastards down on the streets.

***

Stacy

Hilton Hotel

Dunwoody, GA

As I paced around listening to these assholes complain about what they did wrong for the thirtieth time, I finally stood to my feet to add my two cents in the bullshit. We were back in the city looking for blood, and one motherfucker specifically. The dog ass nigga T, and I wasn't gonna be satisfied until I hunted his ass down for the finishing title. I dreamed of the day I could make him pay for killing my husband, and making me suffer, but part of me knew it was my fault for even sneaking around with him in the first place. It was a time where I needed comfort Fresno wasn't able to give, a comfort only T could give me at the time, and I regretted it with every day that passed. But now that my revenge was in Chino's hands, it was probably gonna be impossible to see a true satisfaction rise from this dick head handling anything.

"Could you idiots just please, shut the fuck up!" I looked around at all of them sitting around, fussing about a problem that none of them had yet to solve.

"What the fuck do you mean, shut the fuck up? We been busting our ass trying to make this shit happen for you." Chino looked up at me with a nasty grin.

It was three other loose-mouth flunkies sitting around him. All was paid over ten grand apiece to have T and his son murdered within days, so we could head back to Alabama and split the rest of the take. But it was starting to seem like more of our men were dying at the hands of the same fools we came to get rid of, and I was truly dissatisfied with the results.

"How the fuck are you doing this for me, when I asked for simple requests? Our mission was to come and kill T, take these bitches off for their money, and make it back to Alabama in time to celebrate this fuckman's demise for killing my husband. It doesn't seem like that has yet to take place. So, who are the fucking suckas here, because it damn sure doesn't look like T's people. Why isn't this motherfucker dead yet?"

"Maybe because these niggas is everywhere, and we chasing a whole fucking neighborhood and not the guys we were paid to kill," one of my guards answered out of turn.

Before I could even breathe again, my right backhand was colliding against his eye. His head twisted harshly before he grabbed his face with a clueless expression.

"Next person that says something sarcastic gets two to the fucking face, and we can end the night there." I reached for my pistol on the on the marble counter, gazing at all of them wickedly.

"Stacy, you need to calm down sis, he can't get handled if you keep trying to get rid of all of us. We're on the same team, remember?"

I ignored his stupid remark and made my way to the center of the room where I could be heard clearly.

"I don't know if you niggas are retarded, or just straight up lost with a brain in your skull. We've been at this for a little too long now, and I'm starting to get impatient. I'll put it this way. Find this piece of shit, handle the business, and let's get back to my comfort zone, before we lose any more of my people to this bullshit. Is that understood?"

"Clear." Chino held up a hand to ensure me I was being heard.

"Now get the fuck out!" I dismissed them all, waving my hand at the door.

Watching them all disperse from my room. I ended up alone, standing at the mini bar, pouring up a drink of tequila. I sipped it slowly, pondering on what I had to do in order to receive my exact revenge without failing, falling to the defeat of the state of Georgia. They were beneath me, and all I wanted was the payback for all I had lost.

After tossing my drink back, I sat back in my own thoughts until a knock sounded off against the hotel's door. I was just seconds from drowning myself in a hot shower, and nothing surely was more important than me ruining T's miserable little life that he was barely holding on to.

Making my way over to the door, I didn't use the peep hole before I opened up, which I was about to regret more than anything I'd done in my life.

"APD! ATF! Get the fuck down!"

A white, freckled-face redneck, towering at about six and a half feet bumped me hard as fuck with his shoulder, forcing me to fall. They were falling inside the room like roaches from Raid spray, guns aimed like I had been ratted out.

Please don't move, ma'am. I will not hesitate to shoot!" the aggressive ass white boy stated with a dedicated expression.

"What the fuck is this, free pick-a-female Thursday, muthafucka? This is a hotel, not a fucking drug house. Why in the fuck am I on the ground like I just murdered somebody!" I was loud as fuck, as the spittle flew from my mouth recklessly.

A brown-skinned suited man, no more than thirty, strolled over to me with a packet of papers bound with a jimmie clip. He scanned whatever the fuck was printed on the other side, but his eyes said he truly didn't care what was about to turn about with me in this hotel room.

"Tracey Willingham. Born and raised in Mobile, Alabama. Turns out to have an outstanding amount of violent charges on the history, even aggravated assaults stacked by the mile. Notoriously known for being the wife of the menace, Fresno, the nastiest scum to ever walk the streets of Alabama. I can't say it isn't an honor to meet you. I'm Detective Tyler Bennett. I think I might have a few warrants out for your arrest also." He shook the papers lightly in his hand.

"Excuse me? I haven't did shit. I've been in Atlanta for a long period of time, so you trying to run the old 'break me' trick about doing something back out that way, you've already lost this conversation. What are the charges?" I spat, looking at him, eyes squinting deeply at his deceiving face.

He chuckled, folding his arms, with a look that said he knew something I didn't. At least, that's what my mind told me when I saw the nasty smirk slide across his face.

"Oh, I can guarantee you you're wanted for charges back down in Alabama, but that doesn't exclude the murders

recovered since you've stepped foot into our city. The shoot-
ings and also the way you're causing chaos in the streets with
the infamous Miami T. They call me Ty. That's the name they
currently know me by. It just so happened as I watched these
scumbags trafficking drugs across the northern border, I realized they were building a strong enough bridge to destroy you
specifically. I'm good with remembering names." He winked.

Two bulky, SWAT officers lifted me from the ground by
my arms, forcing me to gaze this police ass detective in the
eyes.

"I'll tell you this, Ms. Willingham. This will be the only
moment you have to save yourself and walk away from this in
the next few months, or you can play whichever role you
choose, and deal with the stretched prison sentence I'm gonna
slap on the rest of your affiliates. One by one."

"Fuck you, faggot. Make sure you put me in a single cell
until I speak with my lawyer, sucker!" I shouted, trying to
jump and headbutt his weak ass.

He took a small step back, and nodded for them to carry
me away, because I was quickly snatched off my feet and being toted out of the hotel room. I kicked and screamed like an
innocent citizen, but I knew the tar was about to get stickier,
regardless of what avenue I decided to take.

Detective Bennett slid one last comment towards me before the elevator opened, and cuffs clinked down on my wrist.

"I hope your husband's death was worth this filthy drug
war that's on your hands, because you will be buried in it by
the next time you see me," he said, calmly walking off.

I swallowed spit, knowing the tables had just gotten past
ugly. The slightest of evidence could plant me in prison for
life, and I honestly had no way to cover my tracks with the
sneaky ass state of Georgia, hounding the courtroom to ille-
gally pick me out as the criminal. It was beyond T. All of them

had to die, whatever he loved, because witnesses were not gonna have a chance to spin the cards on me. *All I needed is the phone,* I thought as the elevator doors closed up.

I was escorted quickly through the lobby, where more undercovers crept around, and directly outside to a Silver Expedition. Within the next twenty minutes, I was being booked into Fulton County Jail, and immediately out housed to Union City's County Detention Center.

Chapter 12

East Atlanta

Smokey

I was driving in a new rental. The all-black Jaguar was sliding smoothly through the streets. I knew it was early enough in the afternoon to catch One Leg Don out and about around the four-way, or posted on Bouldercrest, where he showed his face every other week or so. It was sewn up tight with the work as in hustler clientele, and his people were the ones to blame.

It was crazy that we had to step up to every major factor in order to distribute some slight understanding, because their press was squeezing every dollar out of the consumers, but Blue wasn't able to move his supply any quicker, when a chain was on the front door. One Leg Don was gonna have to be the access into letting me divide the pie with kindness, where we all left with a smile, or we were gonna be the only ones able to smile.

"Isn't that him right there?" Keith pointed lightly in the passenger seat.

His brother Echo was in the back on full alert, and it took me a second to adjust my eyes correctly, but he was damn sure accompanied with another nigga, sliding inside Langford's Barbershop.

"You damn right that's his ass." I quickly made a U-turn, pulling inside the section from the farthest driving lot.

Parking the car at least twenty-five feet away from any cameras spotting our tags, Echo and I checked our guns simultaneously, and stepped out the car behind Keith.

"I need you to be smooth, dawg. You been making these folks feel there isn't an option when there is, bro. Allow them

111

to walk with us before you go off the handle." He gave me a cautious gaze before we gained our vision of the glass door we approached.

"Whatever you say, man. I just know how these cats get down now. These old heads like him from the east side would rather die before you say your mission got accomplished. I just wanna make sure that option never gets to be placed into thought," I replied back calmly.

His head rotated to Echo, who seemed to be more excited, than the usual businessman.

"You neither, nutshell. Remain calm."

"I haven't uttered a word, sir." He grinned with a shrug.

Before another word could be spoken, Keith was opening the entrance door, walking inside with our feet nearly walking up his back pants legs.

One Leg Don and his little buttmate were both occupying a chair, preparing to get a clean cut. It was even more weird because they were the only two inside the entire shop, besides the two barbers that prepped them up.

Keith strolled calmly over to them, and almost went unnoticed until one of the clipper men cleared his throat, tapping One Leg Don's shoulder.

He cut his eyes up at us with silence, but gave a half-smile, seeing me and Keith.

"Fellas, how ya feeling today? I see y'all out an about, getting some of this good ole wind. He rested back in the seat, with no indication of fear on him.

"Nah, not really, big man. We came to talk about some business and need it to blow smooth like the wind. It's a slight better theory than feeling it, with all respect." Keith shrugged lightly.

Me and Echo stood behind him, looking like we were ready to maul on whatever moved, and the barbers quickly felt the tension slowly rise.

"Look, I'ma be honest, Don. The streets have been abused for the past few months, and it seems like it's getting harder every day to push through the slippery slopes we've been falling in. Blue asked us to do a round-up and get a few people to look into shopping with us on our product."

"And let me guess, I popped up on you fellas' list?" Keith huffed with light aggravation, before smiling with a nod.

"Yeah, you did."

One Leg Don laughed as the barber began to cut his hair, as if the statement that was just mentioned didn't mean a thing.

"Tell Blue I'm not interested. This isn't the old days where you can scare me into doing anything. Let alone push up on me like I'm some type of small-time ass street punk with an extortion plan. Maybe you niggas can come work for me if things have went downhill for my mans, because we getting the load over here. Y'all kids find something safe to do, please."

It was hard for me to hold my composure, and my eyes rotated to Keith for answers on how to proceed. Time was running out, and we had no ounce of knowledge for how we would have our entire movement back off the ground, before the next couple of weeks slid through.

Keith waved his hand towards me for my choice of action to simmer down before I made a mistake, and that's when I saw Echo's gun sliding from his waist. He aimed at One Leg Don's security, firing one slug into the center of his head.

Bocc!

The men instantly started to panic, and move out of scariness, which forced Echo to gun both of the barbers down one by one.

113

Boc! *Boc*! *Boc*! *Boc*! *Boc*!

I watched them crumble to the floor like two sheets drenched in water, and I had to say I knew for sure Echo was a true gremlin within Keith's family. After killing the three men, he placed his gun back on the hip, allowing Keith to approach closer to One Leg Don, who still remained in the chair shaking with fear.

"I'm not sure you met my brother, but as you can see this is the type of nonsense he brings to our agreements. I didn't expect you to deny us, because this is the reason we rise in this type of game, Don. Unity. We have supply that we need sold, and I'm afraid now, you don't have a choice how it will work out in your behalf. We want everything you make, and I'm not gonna have to stick around in order for you to oblige. We will be back in one week to collect. Anything else outside the guidelines of what we explained… do you have any questions?" Keith asked him with a serious mug as if the answer we wanted would switch.

He was shaking so bad he could barely get the yes from his mouth. Echo tapped his jaw lightly to force out what we needed to hear.

"I-I understand. I do."

"Good, because the next time, we won't understand. You make sure you and your buddies here have a great day. Like I said. Next week. Same time."

Making our way to the exit door, Echo tucked his gun as we walked back into the bright sun. Keith turned his head towards him with a disapproving smirk.

"I asked you to stay calm, dick head."

"I tried. That was like three minutes of calmness back there. You should have felt how hard it was to pull that trigger, man." Echo smiled.

I was still lost for words, but I knew I couldn't change the game plan up after it was already laid perfectly for us. We were about to go against the entire city to see the plan Blue had risen higher than the sky.

"So, what the fuck do we do now, because if we go through the hood killing everything that doesn't coincide with us, we might eventually have a problem on our hands."

Keith climbed into the front seat and looked over at me when I got in the passenger seat.

"We're gonna move smoothly and lock this city down, piece by piece, until we got in our palms. It's nearly at the end with the mission, and I can see us paying off Rhestay within the next two weeks, if we are quick enough with the press for these blocks. We have to make sure this is the last time we have to show our faces like this. It's the way I see it."

I listened to his theory and knew it was bound to come up with a bridge somewhere, with all the pandemonium we were causing. I just didn't know how it would come about. If we didn't get rid of our enemies in time, we were probably gonna be laying in a casket before our come-up could transpire. I didn't want to perish from the cause of the almighty dollar, but it seemed like being knee deep in the game was gonna drown us, before we had a chance to make it out.

"Who the fuck are you?" the menacing voice of an older man shouted through the crack of the glass.

I couldn't make out a face, but business was obviously closed for that night. It was strange, and the usual crowd that Infested the area was nowhere in sight.

"Damn bro, I thought I'd stop by for some fucking food, the sign says you shut down at eleven."

"All orders go through the back after nine, smart guy," he responded walking away from me as if I were the new jack of the block.

It would've been a miracle if I could catch Miami T myself and slang him straight back to prison for bringing the fucking heat to the city. Feds were finally involved, and shit was about to turn big."

Making my way around the large building, I maneuvered between a couple of parked cars and found a empty lot and the small burglar bar door. I nearly jumped from my skin when the captain stepped out of the darkness into my view. His gun was aimed at my chest from his right hand, and before I could flinch, the flash of the gun rang through my ears like a bass drum.

***

Stacy

Union City Detention Center

After I was booked in the weak ass county, I'd gotten my call for the stupid ass nigga Chino to come bail me out and couldn't even get an answer. This was supposed to be my husband's brother, family, a so-called nigga you could depend on. But all the time as I tried to preach before, he was not fucking reliable.

Walking through the small corridor with an officer, I was told I had an attorney visit, and had yet to speak to a representative, so I knew it had to be the cops. It was easy to pick the brain of a cornbread Georgia head, and I refused to let them catch me on a humbug like this. I was gonna make my exit, and strike with my business before this city knew it. It was unstoppable.

Stopping at a white steel door in the center of the hallway, I was escorted in and left to the presence of a white-haired man with a tailored black suit. He wore a pair of black leather gloves, and stripes were on his trench coat, indicating he we probably the superior.

"Stacy, should I call you?" He folded his arms, smile drizzling with sarcasm.

"Guess you should." I shrugged with a nasty grin.

His posture never changed an inch, neither was he fazed by my comment.

"I'll say this one time, and one time only. I have the power to bury you alive in the state of Georgia for the rest of your natural life. Your kids and relatives will be praising your name for the time you suffer in a cell, until every breath in your bones suffered to the end. I came here to offer you a deal. As the Captain of Dekalb County, I would like to see my little problem that you're having come to an end, immediately. You have a similar issue, and I would agree if all it would just silence out like a smooth night in a cabin. I need a cut in everything you've got, and I'll let you out with your freedom to handle your pest and proceed out of my state. How's that sound?" He leaned forward with a sinister look.

I knew he was referring to T, and the fact of him knowing even half of my business made me know shit was more than serious. I didn't hesitate to bite the bait.

"You don't have to bribe me, sir. Whatever the cost, isn't a problem. Plus, my issue was still in the making, regardless of interference. I'm guessing you're the assistant my husband referred about to me in the past. So, you know the personal intention for why I'm here, correct?" I slowly stood up to face him in the large glass window.

"Oh, I know and if I didn't, I wouldn't be here. All I know is you've made dirty money in my city, while these bodies have been dropping, and I say four hundred grand of it needs to drop my way tomorrow, or you won't make it have revenge for anything but a shower rape."

"Deal. Where do I need to have my people show?"

"I'll be in touch with whom I choose, I know who you all are. If it's not done my way, it's gonna crumble, just to let you know. I know exactly who you are, and what you're capable of, but I'm gonna let you know I have the last stomp on the grounds of Atlanta. I hope we got that understood."

I nodded with a smile, winking.

"I've understood every word, boss. You have my full attention, so don't think that I'm allowing it to go to waste."

"Good, because if doesn't goes right, I'll make this more than wrong for you. Thanks for your time, Ms. Stacy. A guard will be down to escort you back in a minute," he responded, before walking out the door behind him.

Standing in the room alone, my mind was going back to when Fresno introduced me to our business in Atlanta, and how I was gonna have to work my keys to get around. Well, I was about to demonstrate the art of playing with family, to end my quest in the shitty state. Once I tasted a way, all gas was pushing down that lane, and I wasn't stopping for mercy.

Chapter 13

Blue's Home

Smokey

Arriving back around Blue's home later on that night, I pointed at the pearl-white Mercedes Benz in the driveway. It was only one person I knew rolled in the same car, with two exact cars to match and that was Rhestay.

Stepping out of the car, Keith headed straight for the door, and I followed without a word. Echo trailed directly behind me. Walking inside, we slowly came around to the living room, where Rhestay sat with two of his guards, and Blue sitting calmly in the single leather chair with a pissed expression.

"If it isn't the two that still fuck around like punk faggots with all the money that still owed to me, mon. I think we were just ending this conversation about you two, but I'm not sure if I'm just dumb or talking to a bunch of special kind of men."

"Your insults have been made numerous times in my home since you've been here, Rhestay. Your opinion can fly wild, but your disrespect will not continue. Mind your tongue," Blue interrupted him with a stern voice.

He chuckled, with a raised arm at Blue, pointing his finger. "I gave you everything, and your feelings float because I feel salty about your business. It's been this way since the introduction of us doing business, so I could care less about the anger. Your young kin is the reason for the downsize of our procedure, and I hold you responsible." He stood to his feet, flipping the collar to his snakeskin Gucci jacket.

"Well, business doesn't have to proceed. I think you're confused on me needing your business and wanting to do any purchasing from you." Blue stood up next.

119

Keith quickly walked over to intervene and held up his hand.

"Wait, Rhestay, it's not Blue's fault. We—"

"Have fucked up numerous times. fool. Fuck your excuses! Have my money in a week, or we will have more than bad business on our hands."

"Is that a threat to my nephew?" Blue stepped forward.

Keith placed his hand against Rhestay's chest when he jumped towards Blue, and my eyes watched one of his guards reach for his waist. Before I could think on reacting, I pulled my gun and put a bullet through his head.

Boom!

Rhestay's second guard opened fire towards us, forcing me to take a dive behind the couch, before he rushed his boss to the front door to exit.

Bloc! Bloc! Bloc! Bloc!

I tried to shoot back, but the bullets were whistling past my head and before I could get right, they were already clear from the house, and jumping into the cars parked outside.

Stumbling to my feet, I immediately placed eyes on Keith helping Blue up to his feet. I made my way over, still with my pistol aimed, regardless of the dead Bahamian laying on his floor.

"Are you guys alright?" I looked at Blue breathing hard with a pissed look.

I knew I probably had fucked up pulling the burner, but I truly didn't know what to do. It was either kill or be killed, but at that time I knew I had just created an entirely new problem.

"I'm sorry, Blue." I held my head down, pondering on what the fuck to do.

"It's okay." He shook his head, waving his hand. "You saved my life, and I should be thanking you. I'm afraid we have to get away from here though. This right here has opened a door for chaos and we can't remain here after crashing with Rhestay."

"What do you want us to do?" Keith and Echo looked at him with patient faces for a response.

"Allow our people to make our money and leave the scene for good right now. No hustling. We need these clowns dead, and that's what has to happen. Send them out to take care of these idiots, or we won't have an establishment to run before it's all said and done. I'll call a few of my people. We're moving tonight." Blue walked off, heading for the second floor of the house.

"I have to place a few more calls to put our people on point, 'cause I got some good leads on these suckas. I don't know how to come about with this Rhestay thing though." I looked over to Keith with a clueless expression.

He grabbed his car keys out of his pocket and walked over to the desk in the far right-hand corner, pulling a pistol from inside.

"We do exactly what we said first. End this shit and take what's ours. I've come too far to pass our seats up, so if we gotta delete the plug in the mix to stay afloat, it's done. Place three hundred grand on his head, and if we catch him first, finish the argument to where it can never grow loud again. It's too late to lose focus," he said with a straight face.

"But what the fuck we about to do now?"

"We're about to do what we do best. Turn our names upside down in the city." He nodded for us to follow him, stopping Echo at the door. He lowered his gaze. "Not on this one, lil bro. Unc needs your protection and help. Me and Smokey will take care of this issue, while you make sure Blue is secured. I can't have you back out here like that. Trust me."

Echo looked like he wanted to disagree, but the face that Keith was making showed exactly how much he meant what he just said.

"Whatever you say, man." He folded his arms, standing in the doorway, as we proceeded out to the driveway.

Getting to the car, Keith stared me in the eyes. I knew his mind was in a thousand places.

"However this turns out, we're not coming back until this is settled. Whoever isn't with us when we leave this driveway will have to see why we're the ones to be the last standing. Nothing else matters."

"Let's handle it and see what's next. I'm right here until you say we walk away," I stated to let him know I had his back line hundred percent.

Climbing in the car, we swerved from the driveway to stain the streets with more trouble, in order to show who were the true bosses of the drug game. The crown was for the taking, and I was riding until our team held it in the air.

***

Mama Vee

Making my way inside the Greyhound station with all my babies in front of me, I checked in at the counter to make sure all of our tickets were in order. It was hard when it came down took a decision that toyed with my heart, but I had no other choice but to do what was best for my children, and the safety of the family. The danger was too serious with T and Smokey, so I decided to go live with a few family members in California, until we came down to a resolution of them stepping away from the game.

We'd failed ourselves with happiness, the ordinary lives of just being family, and accepting the days the good Lord graced upon us for the love of the money. I could see them drowning in their own demise, and it was killing me slower than cancer from the nicotine in a cigarette. I couldn't bear losing them, so I transitioned to make my way far as possible from them before I had no brains left to think with at all. It was corruption all over Atlanta, and I knew they were bound to get swallowed in it headfirst if they didn't adhere to the signs.

I bought a few snacks at the vending machine and took a small nap with them as we waited for our first bus to arrive at the station. We had to travel on another Greyhound, and also catch a plane from the surrounding airport to make it out to my family's home in time. Just as I heard the number to our bus pulling into the station, I shook all of them from their sleep, and looked up to see T standing in front of me, out of nowhere. His hoodie was over his face, and he stared at me without saying a word.

I ignored him as if he wasn't even present and continued to gather the kids' things, as they stared around in confusion. I knew the only ones who probably had an idea of what was occurring was OJ and Chris, but I didn't even want them to ponder too much on why I was making my decision. T began to hug them all silently with a kiss to the forehead.

"So, you just gonna disappear on me, and take them from me as if I deserve this, Vee? I'm only trying to protect our family. Don't you get that?" He stepped closer to me as I prepared to walk off.

"Your actions show me exactly what you're trying to do, T, and you're also showing me that you're choosing the streets over us. We can't with every battle that's presented. We can't become the richest family on the planet, because there's people that have already filled those spots, T. Don't you get it? This can only go one way for us. So, I'm doing what I need to so our kids won't have to see you get buried. Does that make enough sense?" I clutched all the bags, trying to walk around him the opposite way.

He stepped back into my lane, embracing me in a tight hug.

"I will be up there with you, but if I don't end this now, we probably will never be a family like you want to have. I wouldn't do anything to risk you leaving my side, not after all we've been through. I hope you get that, Vee." He pecked the side of my lips sincerely. I wanted to slap his ass so bad for what I was being put through, but I just couldn't put up no more of a fight.

"We'll be waiting on you and Smokey in California. If you guys aren't there in two weeks, I'll know exactly what means more." I brushed the kids in front of me, so we could get outside to our bus. "Let's go, y'all. Stay together." I made my way outside the double doors. I watched T follow me and prayed no one else was watching, because I knew he was probably wanted by every street thug, or police officer on the street.

Loading all my children on the bus, we got seated and I stared out the window at the man that used to be my husband. I didn't know if I would be able to touch him again, nor see him for whatever our love was worth. It was time to end a rough chapter in my life, and I wasn't looking back for nothing.

As the bus pulled away my kids waved to their father, and I sat back in my seat, closing my eyes for some form of peace. No matter how much my mind tried to force them out of my head, I couldn't. The pain was only going to rise higher as the days continued is all my heart screamed, as I thought about T and Smokey laying in a casket.

Chapter 14

Chino

It was early the next morning when I cracked my eyes, with anger still flushing through my body like a bad disease. Stacy was sitting inside of a jail, and now I was being forced to meet a crooked ass cop my brother trusted and left in the mix of our business. My only reason for even agreeing was the fact of getting Stacy out of confinement, so we could handle our situations, and clear our way back to Alabama, before we ended up on the most wanted news station. My head was flipping a thousand summersaults, as I moved around the duck-off spot, with my shooter posted in the living room waiting for my command on what was next for us.

"Do you think we need to lay low until we get word on what's going on out there? That would be ugly if we really got the police out for our head with a set-up. Were gonna blow a whole mission on the strength, and probably get our ass handed to in court when they book us." He spoke his mind like he had been holding that shit in for the last few hours or so.

"Nigga, it ain't no other choice. If I don't meet with these motherfuckers, Stacy might not make it to tell us what's next, so right now I'm thinking for everybody. We lay the press down for the last of this cash, and dead these fuck niggas that's having this duck-duck goose chase with us. If we can't, we slide and let it die down until we can double back, and finish it then," I explained as I zipped the duffle up and tucked my 9mm on my waist.

He sat looking absent-minded as if my words were slightly misunderstood, but eventually nodded like he was agreeing to my next plan.

"Ay, look man, we ain't gotta switch nothing but a few things, and keep sliding the way we have. We bound to catch Smokey and T sooner than expected, and that's gonna be the day we sit back and live like bosses for the rest of our natural lives. Our overseer has paid a lot of money to see these suckas stop breathing, and Stacy ain't gonna stop on the strength of Fresno. We hold the ball. But we damn sho can't second-guess it." I looked him in the eye, trying to see what he was acting so nervous for.

"I hear you, fool. You right." He chuckled, wiping the side of his face.

"Nigga, I don't know if you still sleepy, but I need you woke out here. Let's go ahead and snatch up this other bread, so we can go post this bail." I grabbed my keys, heading for the door.

My shooter Laz walked out before me, stepping out into the blazing sun and active neighborhood. I locked the door and quickly followed walking to the car. There was a little traffic on the street, and a few neighbors out and about, taking in the mellow afternoon air. I placed my vision to the ground when I got to the curb where my car was parked and jumped from the loud gunshot that rang out.

Boom!

I caught the bullet slapping Laz in the side of the head, knocking his brain through the side of his head. His body collapsed to the concrete, and my heart reacted quicker than my brain. I snatched my pistol from the hip, letting shots recklessly off around me, as I broke across the street through a neighbor's driveway.

Bop! Bop! Bop! Bop! Bop! Bop!

Even with me falling and shooting for my life, I could hear the return fire popping, and the bullets were flying past my head like jets. Some said I was about to die, but I managed to take cover on the side of the house and stopped to send another four shots at whoever the fuck was creeping down on me.

Bop! Bop! Bop! Bop!

A bullet slammed into my arm, forcing me to drop my gun and take off running up the side of the house, for whatever escape route I could.

"Fuckkk. Aghh, fuck!" I grunted in pain, trying to hold the blood starting to leak from the wound. I could hear more gunshots letting loose as I reached the brown, ten-foot gate. Without hesitation all my pain subsided, and I leaped for the top, flipping straight over that bitch and landing on my back. I nearly lost my wind and dropped a tear from the excruciating pain quaking in my right arm. Running through a section of sticky bushes, I ducked and high stepped for my life. I felt my heart beating like an old subwoofer, but my legs wouldn't stop pushing.

Finding myself exiting through another yard on the following two streets over, I quickly jogged over to the store, and made my way inside the filthy looking bathroom sitting on the side of the building. Traffic was still moving smoothly, and I ducked off in the shit house unnoticed. Falling against the wall, I reached up, locking the door. I was breathing harder than a dog that had been raced on the hound track.

Ripping my shirt, I wrapped it tightly as I could around my forearm to stop my blood from spilling. I didn't know what the fuck had just happened. Neither did I know who was just trying to gun me the fuck down. All I knew is I barely escaped with my life, and I wasn't about to get taken out that soon.

Standing to my feet, I rinsed hot water over my bloody hands, and quickly tried to clean myself up from looking like I just committed a murder. I sat in front of the mirror pondering on what the hell I had to do. I knew if I ran across anyone from this point on that didn't come with me, I was killing and asking questions later. I had to get across town to another gun, and the money we'd been striking for since we arrived in Atlanta.

Tossing all the bloody clothes and tissue into the metal trash bin, I slowly opened the door, peeking my head out. Stepping back into the sun, my eyes spotted an empty Impala parked at the gas pump, and to make it better, the engine was purring like a lion as if God was passing me the way out.

Not hesitating, I pranced over and jumped straight in the driver's seat. Smashing off, I came out the lot of the store like a bat, heading in the opposite direction of my recent run-in. I had no option but to play dirty to ensure we made it out of the bullshit alive. I was prepared to take everybody out, just to stamp my point that we weren't laying down.

Chapter 15

Keith

We were shifting gears with our duties and playing chess, in order to put the disaster to rest. My uncle was now in the outskirts of McDonough, GA, and I was placing everything in order to see that he didn't have to move an inch to see it all form back together. We were stashing shipments in the new attic, and Blue was ordering calls around in search for blood against anyone that came up suspicious on his list. Extra security was hired to guard the house at all times. Six men and eight cameras to watch the surroundings twenty-four-seven. He was stationed off in a new six-bedroom, two-car garage home. It was enough space to fit a fifteen-member family, including a basketball court out back, and another acre of gated land. It was gonna be impossible pulling up to his residence without catching every bullet the shooters had to offer.

In the mix of him telling us his thoughts on moving around. His cell rang, forcing him to pause the conversation. "Speak," he answered calmly.

"You disappoint me, Blue. Me placed trust into you, and you repay me by allowing your people to try and murder me. I hope you've plotted out your funeral, because all you pussies will soak in your own blood, you fucking idiot," Rhestay's voice boomed through the line.

Standing right next to Blue, I could hear his thick accent, and from the look on my uncle's face, he wasn't feeling what was being said. I watched his foot tap lightly in aggravation as he listened to whatever it was dancing through his eardrum.

"Rhestay, first off, you've disrespected me with your filthy insults numerous times. I was starting to actually lose whatever position me and you truly stood firmly in front of,

129

when you began to force your power on me as if I'm a peasant. When in reality, you're a fucking lowlife to me. See, it's one thing you're forgetting. Georgia is my state, Atlanta is my city, and I held it in my palms before you ever stepped your little foreign feet on this turf.

"The altercation the other night was caused from your guard reaching in the midst of a heated incident. In line, my young hustler did what he felt was best, and now we are ready to throw some funds in for your killer's funeral. It's the only truce I can form in my head when you overstepped boundaries, not me," Blue spoke through the line without a sign of shakiness in his tone.

Rhestay began to curse loudly again, and I could see Smokey trying his best to tune in, but nothing was able to be heard as Blue walked smoothly over to the corner to keep all ears deaf from what was about to occur. I knew I wasn't going anywhere in the midst of all the threats he was shouting, and the paranoia of having to watch our backs was more than serious now. We were actually at odds with the same man that supplied us for the last eight years. He was oblivious to the lengths we could reach, and before anyone stomped on the floor we stood on, we were gonna shake the ground like a pitbull locked on a rabbit.

"I'll be clear when I say this, Rhestay. We have bad blood in the air. I'll take this moment to walk away from our differences and call it all even. But if you force my hand, we will have war. That's law, and I will crush you," Blue spat, with a vein protruding from his neck.

I knew he was at his peak, and the look that settled in his pupils was one I've never seen my entire life of being around him. Whatever Rhestay replied with, Blue hung up the line and walked back over to us.

"What's the word? Do we have a bigger problem on our hands?" I questioned, praying we didn't have to go toe-to-toe with the Bahamian. Of course, he was powerful and had connections all around, but we were just as plugged as he could be. The meaning for war caused money to decrease, bodies to fall, and even worse, the police to start creeping and learning names that was supposed to be held under the water.

"I don't care what he said. I'm with you all the way, Blue. I feel all that has happened revolves around me, and I'm willing to lay my life on the line. We've gotten too far, and if I have to put a bullet through his head myself, consider it done," Smokey butted in with his true feelings pouring out.

My uncle moved over to him, embracing him in a hug and tapped his index finger against my friend's temple.

"You are smarter than you know, and I appreciate your loyalty since you've been on board with me and my nephew, for my entire establishment. You're family now, so whatever you feel, we feel. If we move, we move together. There is no such thing as you risking yourself."

I stood quietly, listening to him as he turned and walked over to the computer sitting on the cherry oak top. He sat calmly down in his seat and began typing something on the keyboard.

Me and Smokey stood back waiting for his next order. It was a few minutes later when he ceased his typing, standing back up to his feet.

"We are at war with Rhestay now, so anything that was owed to him is paid in full, and we will also answer with blood. Lots of blood. I just contacted a few friends of mine to assist with this problem, friends that dedicate their time to torture, pain and demise for the cause of me. I want you two to maneuver around, and close down shop wherever we have them open. Collect, and inform everybody that has linked with us, there is no switching. We will supply them all in full, and anyone that thinks of selling on our turf will perish." He folded his arms with confidence.

"So, is this it for our faces being shown? It's like we're gonna have to stay low key forever," I asked, wondering how things may play out for us, if the pigs got involved. We were on a mission to be the plugs of Atlanta, but it came with so many obstacles, it was liable for us to slip at any moment.

"We will take three more weeks of pressing down our force in this city and relocate to New York to open up new houses. We will run the city from other hands, and head street runners in charge of certain sections. If one slips and betrays us, he will die, and the entire crew under him as well. To make sure your faces don't get mixed in the turmoil, keep yourselves out of the streets during the day. Move at night and make it back to our quarters immediately. Welcome to the dope game." He looked at both of us and walked out of the meeting room.

I took a minute to think about what he just laid on us. It was crucial on what Smokey had gotten involved with, and the thought of his family weighed heavy on my mind.

He faced me, holding out his hand. His eyes were teary, but he didn't drop a single drip down his face.

"I don't know what you got on your mind, bro, but I'm with that shit… however it turns out, I'll know it was real."

Shaking his hand, I nodded, respecting the man he had grown into since our bid in juvenile. He was the definition of a real friend. A brother I could trust with my life and that was enough for me.

"Let's take our city." I smirked.

Chapter 16

Guy

It was around midnight when I got released from Dekalb County Jail. I took my way out and I couldn't say I was proud of it, but I would rather it be the fools on the street before it was me. I was limited in my movements, and I had a few places to snatch up some owed cash, but I wasn't about to wait around for one of the hooligans to find me. I was about to take what I could and skip town before the big sweep came. I didn't want to be no way around, neither did I want anyone getting suspicious of my name.

Arriving at Overlook Atlanta Apartments, I slid to the back until I reached my lil chick Marcy's spot. She had been working at the Social Security Office for a while, but for the last few weeks while I was in the slammer, I couldn't get her to answer. I didn't know if she was okay, because I never went without a pick-up, regardless of attitudes or differences. It was the closest place I could go without anyone on the lurk for me, plus a woman's comfort was all I could really trust embracing me with calmness.

Knocking on her front door, I waited patiently, walking in circles. After a few seconds, I placed three more firm knocks on the door. Just when I thought I was stuck and had to replot my avenues, the front door unlocked and opened.

Marcy was standing in front of me in her pink Coach pajamas. Bags under her eyes and her expression, gave me the indication she may had been sick from a cold or something.

"Baby, what the fuck? Are you okay?" I pulled her in for a hug and kiss.

She moved her head slightly with a dissatisfied mug.

"Guy, I'm sick, and you don't need to be catching nothing behind me. I'm in pain, boy." She took a step back.

"Damn boo, I'm sorry, but I'm here now. I'm gonna take care of you, but we have to talk. We really need to be preparing to get out of here." I grabbed her hand, pulling her into the apartment.

The living room was blacked out from the velvet curtains, and no sound could be heard inside but the movement of our bodies. Sitting down on the couch beside her, I rubbed her chin.

"I got some real serious problems over my head, so staying in Atlanta is really coming to an end. But I want you to leave with me. It doesn't matter where as long as I'm with you."

"Leave Atlanta? Guy, what the hell happened now? I can't just up and leave here, Atlanta is all I know. What if you can't protect me?" She turned her gaze looking towards the wall as if doubt was clouding her mental.

"But I can protect you, Marcy. You will be watched over twenty-four-seven, and every move you take, I will take."

"I wonder, can I take that move with y'all, cause I'm damn sure involved right?" I heard a male's voice that sounded too familiar behind my neck.

Turning my head like an owl, Miami T stood in the hallway, pointing two chrome pistols towards me sternly. I could see his trigger finger dancing around the release switch as if he wanted to shoot me before stating his peace. I couldn't move or budge, I couldn't even blink. I gazed at his soulless eyes, beaming down on me with thirst.

"T, wh-what are you doing here?" I asked, hoping he was allowing some form of reasoning for being in front of me, instead of killing me off.

"Oh, you don't know? It seems like the entire east side knows, Guy, even the junkies purchasing sacks from my son's trap spots. You snitched on me, and gave my name to the people, and I got all the info how. It's amazing what niggas behind the wall will dig up, just for a little bit of commissary money on the books. We have unfinished business, Guy!"

I cut my eyes over to Marcy, sitting a few feet away from me, and she couldn't even match my eyes. Her eyes were downcast, filled with betrayal. It was clear I had been set up, and it was nothing in my mind that would force me to think differently.

"So, you with this, Marcy? I thought we loved each other. We had nothing else but each other." I gritted my teeth in anger.

The force of his pistol swinging, connected with my right jaw, and I could feel it shatter when the steel touched my flesh.

Whack!

"Aggghhh! Wait! Waittt! We can come to a deal, T. I never mentioned your name, but I can tell you everything that was mentioned, word for word. You can even get the money I got saved up, and take it for yourself, if you feeling salty about me dealing with them. You gotta hear me out though, please!" I begged through my lips, trying to fight off the pulsating bumping through my cheek.

"Marcy, get your coat and wait in the car." He nodded towards the door.

She did exactly what he ordered, and finally turned to lay her sight on me before walking out. She wanted to say something but proceeded out with no words to comfort me that shit would be good. Once the door closed behind her, T held the pistols closer to me.

"I'm listening."

I caught my breath to speak, and spoke slowly to ensure I didn't say the wrong thing.

"The police chief is working to see you dead. He wants your head, and he's doing whatever to see it transpire. Your son Smokey is just a free asset to him. A life that he wants just because he reminds him of you so much. I'm not sure about what bad blood has spilled between you two, but it's about to ignite. He has the dealers from the west side, on the list to be raided and sent to prison. He's tackling all of the drug dealers on the east in two weeks, and he's gonna send everybody that has touched a nick of dope to the feds.

"He's out for money and working with somebody. I'm just not sure who it is. He thinks I'm gonna testify in court on all the peddlers on the east side, but I was coming to skip town. That's the truth, T!" I held my jaw shaking, with my adrenaline bumping like a club wall.

He smirked, tilting his head.

"If he's working with somebody, you have to know something 'bout them, even if it's small. What makes your story so believable? How do I know you're not hitting me with what you want?"

"Because I don't want to fucking die, T. You gotta believe me. If I die, he's gonna know you're behind it. He's on your bumper every step, and that's the reason I chose to stay out your lane, and just leave. I'm skipping town, like I told you. Anything between us in the past." I held up my hands, pleading out to his mercy.

He watched me silently for a few seconds, and the corners of his eyes slanted down evilly towards me.

"I'm afraid it is in the past, Guy, and that's the reason I'm gonna make sure it stays there and never comes back," he spoke nastily before releasing the trigger on me recklessly.

Boc! Boc! Boc! Boc! Boc!

Chapter 17

Smokey

It was around nine at night when me and Keith swerved over to the east side to see what all we could lay down before, creeping back towards Blue's. I stopped at the four-way and pulled into the store to fill up the gas tank. After going inside to pay for what we needed, me and Keith stood against the car, soaking in the perimeter with our eyes.

I spotted Sue, a known user, creeping from the back of the store with a brown paper bag in her hand. She looked like she had been fucking, and shooting dope at the same time, cause her hair was a mess, but she never was loose on her conscious. She was one of the sharpest junkies around the way, and never slipped on what she needed to know.

"Smokeyyy! Baby…listen, I got sumn to spill in ya ears real quick. You didn't get it from me."

"What's up, Sue? What's going on?" I pulled out three twenties, placing them in her palm.

She looked both ways like somebody could hear her besides me and Keith and placed a hand over her mouth.

"There's been a slime detective creeping through here in different cars, looking for you and your crew. He's hot on the block, and yo name is spreading like wildfire out here. A detective was just murdered behind the Rib Shack. You need to be careful. You and Leaver the Beaver there." She waved her hand, and walked on about her business.

I stared at Keith, waiting to see what input he had on what was just heard but just like me, he formed a raised brow like we were having the same thought.

"I think we got some sneaky motherfuckers trying to double cross us in some shit we have nothing to do with. I don't trust a fucking soul right about now."

"You took the words right out of my mouth. Felipe said he missed by an inch, but he's staying out there on the hunt, so if he's seen again, he's dead. Now we have to worry about whoever this fucking cop is creeping around in search of me," I said getting back into the driver's seat.

Keith got in, adjusting his seat belt, and I quickly made a detour out to Simone's home. She didn't live far from my destination, and I knew it might never be another time, if I didn't get what I had off my chest right then and there.

Within twenty-five minutes of being on the road, I pulled right into her driveway, killing the ignition.

"Bro, I'll be right back. I only need like five minutes." I held up my hand, getting out the car.

"Somebody's already whipped without the nip, I see." He chuckled.

"Fuck you, white boy." I closed the door in the mix while he was jabbering.

Trailing up the driveway was like magic, because she opened the door before I could even knock, and jumped into my arms. Her hair smelled like lemon shampoo. She wore a pair of thin black sweats, and a white T-shirt. Besides the reading glasses she wore, everything was still looking the same. Magnificent.

"Hey, sweetie. How are you?" I laughed, embracing her warm hug back. It ended with her lips meeting mine for a warm interlock, and that was the first time we shared our sentimental moment in the heat of all the drama going on. It was gentle, and I could taste the flavorful bubble gum she had been chewing dance on my tongue.

"It s a surprise to see you here. I was starting to have a few different thoughts about you lately."

"You don't have to think anything about me because I would tell you. I stopped by because I really needed to speak with you about something that's on my conscience, and I don't know how to be nothing but straightforward."

"Is this another episode of you about to disappear again?" She tooted up her nose and wrinkled her face with a look of sadness.

"No, it isn't. It's an act of moving forward. Simone, I'm involved in the streets heavy, and I have a lot of people trying to hurt me, and everybody I love. I'm pushing to plant my feet in the ground until I get enough money to last my next six generations. I'm about to relocate to New York and establish myself in a few weeks. I will still have managers, and employees in charge of my hustling, and we can travel or do anything else you feel you want to." I rubbed her cheek lightly with love running through my veins.

"Of course, I'll go with you. I don't know why you have me so vulnerable, but ever since I've met you, it's like it's my job to ensure you make it out of those streets every night. You're a smart man, Smokey. Too smart to keep making the same mistakes. I would go anywhere with you, because nothing materialistic or valuable means a thing to me. I would rather enjoy the smile I haven't used in a while, and a life where I know you're secured every night," she replied, looking down to the ground beneath her.

I used my finger to lift her chin and gave her a perfect thirty-two smile. I didn't like to see a depressed expression coming from her, and I didn't need any interruptions on what I had planned for her, a family.

"Listen to me, Simone. This way of mine is only to make another day relaxing, and non-stressful. I won't quit until I got enough to last for our next six generations. It's a part of me, and I do it well. I promise to hold you near me with every second we spend together, and I've never did this with a lady, but you've gotten me hypnotized with your spirit, and that's what I want. I don't have to second-guess about that at all," I spoke lightly, while staring into her eyes.

Nothing would make me happier than waking up to a sweet face that I actually wanted to be beside me. I was actually comfortable with risking it all for her alone, that's how much faith I had in my heart for her.

"What if we get there, and you see something different that you want? Your vibe is always so breathtaking and special, I wouldn't want to ruin that by rushing into something you aren't ready for. I'm not that special yet in your eyes, I'm sure." She shrugged, like she was losing her confidence or something.

Kissing her deeply on the lips, I hugged her tightly.

"You are one of a kind, ma. A blessing, I couldn't ask for no better. I'm literally searching for myself and what makes me happy, and that's you. So, pack your things in three weeks, because you're mine for good." I grinned, holding her hand.

She fumbled around with a silly smile for a few seconds, before wrapping me back into a hug.

"I'll go. I hope you know what you got out for you with me every day. I talk a lot." She giggled.

"And that's gonna be my start of learning how to hold twenty-hour conversations. I need you to stay low for a few days, and don't do too much moving. A little more business has to transpire within these next few days, so we can close all open doors. All you have to do is sit patiently for me."

"I'll be right here, Mr., the steps on you." She pointed a finger at my chest and stepped back behind her door. "See you in a few weeks, handsome." Her lips blew me a kiss that made my flesh crawl with emotions.

"Goodnight, love." I turned and headed back down the driveway to the car. Getting in, I started the car, and pulled out slowly.

"You said five minutes, motherfucker. I don't think you can count." Keith looked at me curiously.

"Shut yo ass up, fool. You know this girl got my nose wide open right now. It's spread enough ignorant shit going on, so I wanna lock in every minute I can and bond with her. I'm not trying to be all stiff like you in the next three years." I laughed off my brother's comment.

I knew he could see the joy on my face whenever I was around Simone. Even if this was just a little of time that had been invested, I still made sure to never dedicate myself to nothing with an ounce of my breathing, if it didn't feel it was worth it. I still had yet to feel real love, a connection that I could say was truly only for me. I was tied to the streets with an iron bolt, holding me together firmly. The rush of getting money and stacking dough was implanted in my brain, and I wasn't about to break that motto for anyone. But I definitely wanted to at least gain a queen out of the hard, slanging days I placed into the game. A man was nothing without a queen, and I finally think I had my eyes on the right one.

Pulling up to the next light it flashed red, and I slowed the car to a halt. It wasn't even five seconds later, when a burst of thunder erupted through the sky, sending down a heap of rain. Keith stared out the window as it danced across the glass, silently, as if he was in deep thought.

"Wassup with it? What you thinking about?"

"Life, bro. I mean...what do you think will happen at the end of all this? It's like, sometimes I wonder if I'll ever be able to just make enough money, to the point where I can just hang it up for good. Take care of my wife in another state, or country, and just live for the sake of my children, ya know?"

I gazed over at him with a raised brow because I already knew what was about to come next. Keith wasn't a big speaker on his feelings, but you could read him like a book just from his emotions and words.

"Keith, this is our life. I mean, I didn't have nothing before I met you. I feel like the streets we supply will always look for us to be there, and the times when we can't, they will bash our name for saying we would. It's not like this game was picked by us…it chose us. The operation your uncle Blue has will never have anyone better than you to operate it. I wouldn't give a fuck if you had a cocaine expert. Not me, your brother Echo, or even Rhestay. I don't want to just fold on him in the mix of his rise, but my loyalty is right here because you brought me here."

"I understand, and I respect you for that. I can't just up and leave Blue, even if I wanted to. He stayed beside me when everyone else pushed and left. I'm dedicated to my position, and I will always stand on that. I'm just speaking on another level right now. How long do you really think it will last? Like, is it an end to what we're doing? Or do you feel that we can do it forever with no big stumbles to come? Stumbles we can't get back up from?" He looked at me seriously.

I pushed the pedal, driving smoothly down the two-way street, thinking of every word that just left his mouth. I knew his mind was in a jumble from all the extra chaos that had been going on, plus he never said shit for no reason. I never thought about what I would do if this style of hustling didn't work anymore, and that's when his theory started to turn circles in my mind, because I truly couldn't answer it with a straightforward answer.

Huffing with thoughts beating in my brain, I nodded.

"I get exactly what you're saying bro, and its nothing wrong with thinking ahead for the future. I'm not gonna lie,

Keith. I never thought that far, and it makes me wonder what I will do sometimes. Do I think it would last forever? That's like asking me will I live forever. The answer is no. This game was meant to be taken over, supplied and broken back down, for the next upcoming hustler to build up his foundation through his view.

"I'm only focusing one day at a time because honestly, I can't see the next day with so much going in front of me. It's my dream to run a business or get married with kids, to cherish my family for the rest of my days, but that time will get here when it gets here. Right now, I'm hustling and if I want to keep hustling without tumbling so we can reach that goal, I have to focus. It's the only reason I never go against your word. You're my brother, and I'm not leaving your side, man. When you say it's no more room to be here, that's my word, I'll get out with you. On my mama." I held out a hand, glancing at him for a brief second to show my seriousness.

He stayed quiet for a minute but smiled.

"That's wassup, dawg. That's the reason why I rock with ya the way I do. I guess tomorrow we can try to put the rest of the houses down and prepare to relocate. New York is a big city. Plenty of trouble also, when we talking about setting up shop in a new area. It's just the agenda that comes with it, I guess," Keith replied.

"It does, but as long as we move as one, I don't see nothing, or no one interfering with it. It's always us against them, and that's the way I will always keep it. Period," I added, before placing my attention back on the road.

I knew the game was about to rise for us all, and I didn't have no time to waste. I was ready to embrace it all. I wanted the bread, and I wanted the status to show niggas I don't give a fuck where I was or trapped my product. I would still always remain the fucking plug.

Chris Green

Chapter 18

Mama Vee

Vallejo, CA

It had been fifteen hours since I arrived at my distant cousin's home in Cali. I was so distraught and feeling home sick, especially knowing the two men I cared for deeply might never see me again. It wasn't the fact that I didn't like what they did to provide. I didn't like their decisions to keep pushing the wrong path, once the signs of destruction were showing so vividly. What was I to do as a mother and wife, sit back and let them destroy us? Hell no. It hurt to take off and leave them in the city of Atlanta alone, but I was left with no choice but to protect our young ones until they came to some sense.

It was pulling strings at my heart so bad that I had to step out on the back porch of my cousin's home and try to use the phone to call my son. I knew I could win him over, or even talk some sense into his father. I just prayed he wasn't knee deep, lost to the point where he didn't even feel empathy for my feelings and pleas anymore.

After the first two rings, he picked up with a groggy voice, as if I woke him up.

"Who is this?"

"Your mother."

"Ma? What type of number is this? Are you okay? Why haven't you called me? I've been blowing your cell up since yesterday."

"Smokey, I'm in California. I'm up here with some of our family members, with your brothers and sisters. I left Atlanta yesterday."

"What? Why didn't you tell me? What would make you just up and leave for California?"

"Because I don't want to have to tell your brothers and sisters, I had to bury you and your father for the sake of the streets. Our family was at risk of dying, all for the love of money, so I made the decision that was best for them. That's why, Smokey."

Silence filled the line, but I could hear through the receiver he was getting out of the bed. He exhaled in my ear, and I wanted to scream my anger, but I only knew it would make things worse.

"Ma, first of all, no one is gonna hurt you or my little sisters and brothers. I know things may be a little hard on you, but me and my dad are only trying to ensure that you and them never have to worry or look over your shoulders for anything again. If it was in vain, I would be against every step. But how can I buck on something that's to benefit you? We are the men of our tree, Mama, so it's necessary sometimes to do what he has to."

"No, what's necessary is for you and your father to be alive and with us so we can spend our days together. Money was never an option to me when I married him, or when I had you. It didn't make me change the way I thought or felt, Smokey. So, this isn't for us, it's for you. The game is nasty, and it only ends one way, or one day. It's my fear to get a call that you aren't here anymore. Or, T will never be coming home again, after we waited so long to see Jim make it out.

"Have you thought about how that makes me feel, because I'm having nightmares that's telling me it's coming. You can't beat fate, Smokey. Regardless of what money or name you can earn out there, I raised you to think smart and positive, to be a man of respect and honor. How can you honor me, us, or even yourself for being murdered on the block for wanting to deal a dime bag? Just tell me," I yelled, feeling the emotions starting to come.

"I'm sorry, Mama. But at this point, it's only so much I can actually say. You need all you have, and in order for me to make sure y'all safe, you got to be able to trust our movements just for now. Please," he said as if my mind would change in a matter of seconds.

Part of me wanted to give in and respect the mind frame my son was trying to place upon me, but there was also a side of me saying to remain far away from the devilish aura him and T was giving off. It was like the money and streets had them blinded with a poisonous veil of disbelief. Pushing away further was only going to hurt me, but if it was necessary to not face another devastating moment in my life, then I was willing to take that chance a hundred times again.

"I love you, Smokey, but I expected better of you," I mumbled, hanging up in his ear.

It was going to be a time in my life where I watched everyone leave, and that was when the man upstairs called it to be. I refused to sit around and allow family to show me that another possessed the power to do the same.

***

Rhestay

As I looked out the patio window of my large office, one of my soldiers entered the room, breaking me out of the destructive trance that I had been lost in for hours.

"Bossman, the girl from the states would like a word with you," he whispered, while passing me the phone.

It truly wasn't the time for me to be speaking business, after the situation that lay on my table. Still, I was a man of my word, and business was business. I didn't hesitate to place a plan in effect after the clashing with Blue, and if my services were going to be used in other places, I wasn't about to space the demand of what I wanted first.

"It's good to finally get your call, Stacy. Can't say I'm pleased to speak, but I'm eager to hear whatever you can mix up to soothe me," I spoke deeply into the line.

"Well, I'm sorry to hear it's not a pleasure on your end, because it will never be one of mine. For some reason, I realized I intimidate most people when it comes to this sort of thing, but I will be as gentle as possible. To remind you, these calls are being recorded. Not to say that I give a shit," she replied arrogantly.

"Be careful what you wish, my sister. I'm listening."

"Good. First, I would like you to know I can't be a part of this puzzle, if I'm sitting behind a fucking county wall. It's a must you speak with Captain Williams of the Dekalb Police about me righteously receiving a bond. After that, I need avenues and I mean good avenues, to walk away from this state like the innocent woman I am. Now, your problem? Hmm...let's just say that's minor. You can actually rest your feet up on the La-Z-Boy, if we can move these first few pieces on the chess board. That about sums up any conversation I have for you."

I listened to her speak as if she just was the queen of all queens. I wondered where she ever got the nerve to even open up with a speech as such in my presence. Still, I knew she played a piece in my victory, and that meant more than the small portions that fell for the scavengers to feed off me.

"My end of the bargain is already in place. Once you receive your freedom and step back into the society, remember what is on the table. Because if my business isn't handled accordingly, I'm afraid this recorded phone call wouldn't even have a trace on you. Take that to the cell with you and think about it before you post bail. I'll see you then." I hung up in her face without giving a chance for her to reply.

Gazing over to my two most dangerous hitmen, I smiled. "We have fun to attend to. And I don't want anybody leaving the vicinity after we show up to show how we play, eh? Understand?"

They both nodded in unison, and what was understood didn't have to be repeated. I was placing a ticket on Blue's head for the maximum, and I needed it done at any cost.

Chris Green

Chapter 19

Smokey

After getting the emotional call from my mother earlier that morning, I got out in the wind to blow some steam, and also prepare for our departure to New York. The city was filled with hustlers and killers dedicated on making the last dollar at any cost. I was just the one who refused to leave without ensuring the ones after me were buried deeper than the stones of the Pyramids.

After getting to Uncle Blue's new location for his headquarters. I walked in and made my way to the living room area. Crossing into the threshold, Keith and Blue stood quietly stating at the big screen TV silently.

"What's going on, what the hell y'all watching the numbers for, stocks and bonds?" I joked, knowing that the two was always plotting on business.

Keith gave me a distraught and sour expression, pointing at the TV screen My eyes and ears followed, until they landed on the Spanish woman reporting the latest news for Atlanta city limits.

"In further news today, we have one of the biggest drug indictments that the department has ever seen for the last forty years. District Attorney Paul Steward has tracked witnesses, accomplices, trails of charges and evidence stacked to the roof about the notorious murders, drug trafficking, and money laundering. This wanted group of men has now been charged with by the federal authorities," she said, before a large picture of mugshots hit the main screen. I nearly puked when I saw my face, along with Keith's Uncle Blue, even Felipe's. It was like a moment from the movie *Public Enemy Number One*, but we were actually living the reality now. I couldn't even talk as the woman continued to spill information about the pigs coming for us.

"'These men are labeled dangerous, and we will take all of these criminals down, one by one,' quoted the captain of the police department. We expect to hear more about this on the five o'clock alert, today. This is Jessica Nelson. Back to you."

I was lost for words and judging from Blue and Keith's looks, they didn't know what the fuck to say at the moment either.

"How the fuck did this happen?" I rubbed a hard hand on my head.

Blue started to respond, but before he could get out a word, the large patio door came crashing in, along with the front door. The first thing I spotted was the SWAT team, aiming their rifles with sturdiness.

"FBI! FBI! Get the fuck down on this ground. Now!" Numerous men yelled, catching the three of us by surprise like a deer in the headlights.

We were swarmed by officers within seconds, and slapped into a pair of cuffs, as the leading official spoke through his radio. The weird stare down between me, Blue and Keith told me to remain silent in case anything was gonna be used against us. After a few short minutes of sitting on the floor, Captain Williams from the Dekalb Police Department stepped through the door with a sly smirk on his face. He stepped over to us with arrogance and kneeled down directly in front of me.

"Mr. Carter. You seem to have a familiar name as the man of this city. It's actually an honor to meet you. I may not know too much of all you've done around this state, but after I'm done with you and your little entourage, you'll be cooperating like a homeless guy begging for shelter."

"Fuck you, sucka! What you waiting for? You ain't got nothing on us, pussy," I spat, feeling the anger bubble inside me.

He grinned with satisfaction before nodding at me.

"I guess we just have to see who's bluffing, huh, Mr. Plug of Lil Mexico? Take 'em away." He waved a hand.

The slogan he used on me tingled my nervous button and placed my thoughts in a million pieces. I hope no one was working against us that I didn't have any knowledge of. But with the federal agents busting through the home to see us fall for a major drug operation, this spelled more than just trouble. Shit was probably about to get deeper, and I felt that I was about to disintegrate within.

***

To Be Continued...
The Plug of Lil Mexico 3
Coming Soon

Lock Down Publications and Ca$h Presents assisted publishing packages.

BASIC PACKAGE $499
Editing
Cover Design
Formatting

UPGRADED PACKAGE $800
Typing
Editing
Cover Design
Formatting

ADVANCE PACKAGE $1,200
Typing
Editing
Cover Design
Formatting
Copyright registration
Proofreading
Upload book to Amazon

LDP SUPREME PACKAGE $1,500
Typing
Editing
Cover Design
Formatting
Copyright registration
Proofreading
Set up Amazon account

Upload book to Amazon
Advertise on LDP Amazon and Facebook page

***Other services available upon request. Additional charges may apply
Lock Down Publications
P.O. Box 944
Stockbridge, GA 30281-9998
Phone # 470 303-9761

Submission Guideline

Submit the first three chapters of your completed manuscript to ldpsubmissions@gmail.com, subject line: Your book's title. The manuscript must be in a .doc file and sent as an attachment. Document should be in Times New Roman, double spaced and in size 12 font. Also, provide your synopsis and full contact information. If sending multiple submissions, they must each be in a separate email.

Have a story but no way to send it electronically? You can still submit to LDP/Ca$h Presents. Send in the first three chapters, written or typed, of your completed manuscript to:

LDP: Submissions Dept
Po Box 944
Stockbridge, Ga 30281

DO NOT send original manuscript. Must be a duplicate.

Provide your synopsis and a cover letter containing your full contact information.

Thanks for considering LDP and Ca$h Presents.

<u>NEW RELEASES</u>

THE COCAINE PRINCESS 9 by KING RIO

FOR THE LOVE OF BLOOD 3 by JAMEL MITCHELL

SANCTIFIED AND HORNY by XTASY

THE PLUG OF LIL MEXICO 2 by CHRIS GREEN

Coming Soon from Lock Down Publications/Ca$h Presents
BLOOD OF A BOSS **VI**
SHADOWS OF THE GAME II
TRAP BASTARD II
By **Askari**
LOYAL TO THE GAME **IV**
By **T.J. & Jelissa**
TRUE SAVAGE **VIII**
MIDNIGHT CARTEL IV
DOPE BOY MAGIC IV
CITY OF KINGZ III
NIGHTMARE ON SILENT AVE II
THE PLUG OF LIL MEXICO III
CLASSIC CITY II
By **Chris Green**
BLAST FOR ME **III**
A SAVAGE DOPEBOY III
CUTTHROAT MAFIA III
DUFFLE BAG CARTEL VII
HEARTLESS GOON VI
By **Ghost**
A HUSTLER'S DECEIT III
KILL ZONE II
BAE BELONGS TO ME III
TIL DEATH II
By **Aryanna**
KING OF THE TRAP III

By **T.J. Edwards**

GORILLAZ IN THE BAY V

3X KRAZY III

STRAIGHT BEAST MODE III

De'Kari

KINGPIN KILLAZ IV

STREET KINGS III

PAID IN BLOOD III

CARTEL KILLAZ IV

DOPE GODS III

Hood Rich

SINS OF A HUSTLA II

ASAD

YAYO V

Bred In The Game 2

S. Allen

THE STREETS WILL TALK II

By Yolanda Moore

SON OF A DOPE FIEND III

HEAVEN GOT A GHETTO III

SKI MASK MONEY III

By Renta

LOYALTY AIN'T PROMISED III

By Keith Williams

I'M NOTHING WITHOUT HIS LOVE II

SINS OF A THUG II

TO THE THUG I LOVED BEFORE II

IN A HUSTLER I TRUST II

By Monet Dragun

QUIET MONEY IV

EXTENDED CLIP III

THUG LIFE IV

By **Trai'Quan**

THE STREETS MADE ME IV

By **Larry D. Wright**

IF YOU CROSS ME ONCE III

ANGEL V

By **Anthony Fields**

THE STREETS WILL NEVER CLOSE IV

By K'ajji

HARD AND RUTHLESS III

KILLA KOUNTY IV

By Khufu

MONEY GAME III

By Smoove Dolla

JACK BOYS VS DOPE BOYS IV

A GANGSTA'S QUR'AN V

COKE GIRLZ II

COKE BOYS II

LIFE OF A SAVAGE V

CHI'RAQ GANGSTAS V

SOSA GANG IV

BRONX SAVAGES II

BODYMORE KINGPINS II

BLOOD OF A GOON II

By Romell Tukes

MURDA WAS THE CASE III

Elijah R. Freeman

AN UNFORESEEN LOVE IV

BABY, I'M WINTERTIME COLD III

By **Meesha**

QUEEN OF THE ZOO III

By **Black Migo**

CONFESSIONS OF A JACKBOY III

By Nicholas Lock

KING KILLA II

By Vincent "Vitto" Holloway

BETRAYAL OF A THUG III

By Fre$h

THE BIRTH OF A GANGSTER III

By Delmont Player

TREAL LOVE II

By Le'Monica Jackson

FOR THE LOVE OF BLOOD IV

By Jamel Mitchell

RAN OFF ON DA PLUG II

By Paper Boi Rari

HOOD CONSIGLIERE III

By Keese

PRETTY GIRLS DO NASTY THINGS II

By Nicole Goosby

LOVE IN THE TRENCHES II

By Corey Robinson

FOREVER GANGSTA III

By Adrian Dulan

THE COCAINE PRINCESS X

SUPER GREMLIN II

By King Rio

CRIME BOSS II

Playa Ray

LOYALTY IS EVERYTHING III

Molotti

HERE TODAY GONE TOMORROW II

By Fly Rock

REAL G'S MOVE IN SILENCE II

By Von Diesel

GRIMEY WAYS IV

By Ray Vinci

SALUTE MY SAVAGERY II

By Fumiya Payne

BLOOD AND GAMES II

By King Dream

Available Now

RESTRAINING ORDER **I & II**
By **CA$H & Coffee**
LOVE KNOWS NO BOUNDARIES **I II & III**
By **Coffee**
RAISED AS A GOON I, II, III & IV
BRED BY THE SLUMS I, II, III
BLAST FOR ME I & II
ROTTEN TO THE CORE I II III
A BRONX TALE I, II, III
DUFFLE BAG CARTEL I II III IV V VI
HEARTLESS GOON I II III IV V
A SAVAGE DOPEBOY I II
DRUG LORDS I II III
CUTTHROAT MAFIA I II
KING OF THE TRENCHES
By **Ghost**
LAY IT DOWN **I & II**
LAST OF A DYING BREED I II
BLOOD STAINS OF A SHOTTA I & II III
By **Jamaica**
LOYAL TO THE GAME I II III
LIFE OF SIN I, II III
By **TJ & Jelissa**
BLOODY COMMAS I & II
SKI MASK CARTEL I II & III

KING OF NEW YORK I II,III IV V

RISE TO POWER I II III

COKE KINGS I II III IV V

BORN HEARTLESS I II III IV

KING OF THE TRAP I II

By **T.J. Edwards**

IF LOVING HIM IS WRONG…I & II

LOVE ME EVEN WHEN IT HURTS I II III

By **Jelissa**

WHEN THE STREETS CLAP BACK I & II III

THE HEART OF A SAVAGE I II III IV

MONEY MAFIA I II

LOYAL TO THE SOIL I II III

By **Jibril Williams**

A DISTINGUISHED THUG STOLE MY HEART I II & III

LOVE SHOULDN'T HURT I II III IV

RENEGADE BOYS I II III IV

PAID IN KARMA I II III

SAVAGE STORMS I II III

AN UNFORESEEN LOVE I II III

BABY, I'M WINTERTIME COLD I II

By **Meesha**

A GANGSTER'S CODE I &, II III

A GANGSTER'S SYN I II III

THE SAVAGE LIFE I II III

CHAINED TO THE STREETS I II III

BLOOD ON THE MONEY I II III

A GANGSTA'S PAIN I II III

By J-Blunt

PUSH IT TO THE LIMIT

By **Bre' Hayes**

BLOOD OF A BOSS **I, II, III, IV, V**

SHADOWS OF THE GAME

TRAP BASTARD

By **Askari**

THE STREETS BLEED MURDER **I, II & III**

THE HEART OF A GANGSTA I II& III

By **Jerry Jackson**

CUM FOR ME I II III IV V VI VII VIII

An **LDP Erotica Collaboration**

BRIDE OF A HUSTLA **I II & II**

THE FETTI GIRLS **I, II& III**

CORRUPTED BY A GANGSTA I, II III, IV

BLINDED BY HIS LOVE

THE PRICE YOU PAY FOR LOVE I, II ,III

DOPE GIRL MAGIC I II III

By **Destiny Skai**

WHEN A GOOD GIRL GOES BAD

By **Adrienne**

THE COST OF LOYALTY I II III

By Kweli

A GANGSTER'S REVENGE **I II III & IV**

THE BOSS MAN'S DAUGHTERS I II III IV V

A SAVAGE LOVE **I & II**

Chris Green

BAE BELONGS TO ME I II
A HUSTLER'S DECEIT I, II, III
WHAT BAD BITCHES DO I, II, III
SOUL OF A MONSTER I II III
KILL ZONE
A DOPE BOY'S QUEEN I II III
TIL DEATH
By **Aryanna**
A KINGPIN'S AMBITON
A KINGPIN'S AMBITION **II**
I MURDER FOR THE DOUGH
By **Ambitious**
TRUE SAVAGE I II III IV V VI VII
DOPE BOY MAGIC I, II, III
MIDNIGHT CARTEL I II III
CITY OF KINGZ I II
NIGHTMARE ON SILENT AVE
THE PLUG OF LIL MEXICO I II
CLASSIC CITY
By **Chris Green**
A DOPEBOY'S PRAYER
By **Eddie "Wolf" Lee**
THE KING CARTEL **I, II & III**
By **Frank Gresham**
THESE NIGGAS AIN'T LOYAL **I, II & III**
By **Nikki Tee**
GANGSTA SHYT **I II &III**

166

By **CATO**

THE ULTIMATE BETRAYAL

By **Phoenix**

BOSS'N UP **I , II & III**

By **Royal Nicole**

I LOVE YOU TO DEATH

By **Destiny J**

I RIDE FOR MY HITTA

I STILL RIDE FOR MY HITTA

By **Misty Holt**

LOVE & CHASIN' PAPER

By **Qay Crockett**

TO DIE IN VAIN

SINS OF A HUSTLA

By **ASAD**

BROOKLYN HUSTLAZ

By **Boogsy Morina**

BROOKLYN ON LOCK I & II

By **Sonovia**

GANGSTA CITY

By **Teddy Duke**

A DRUG KING AND HIS DIAMOND I & II III

A DOPEMAN'S RICHES

HER MAN, MINE'S TOO I, II

CASH MONEY HO'S

THE WIFEY I USED TO BE I II

PRETTY GIRLS DO NASTY THINGS

By Nicole Goosby
TRAPHOUSE KING **I II & III**
KINGPIN KILLAZ I II III
STREET KINGS I II
PAID IN BLOOD **I II**
CARTEL KILLAZ I II III
DOPE GODS I II
By **Hood Rich**
LIPSTICK KILLAH **I, II, III**
CRIME OF PASSION I II & III
FRIEND OR FOE I II III
By **Mimi**
STEADY MOBBN' **I, II, III**
THE STREETS STAINED MY SOUL I II III
By **Marcellus Allen**
WHO SHOT YA **I, II, III**
SON OF A DOPE FIEND I II
HEAVEN GOT A GHETTO I II
SKI MASK MONEY I II
Renta
GORILLAZ IN THE BAY **I II III IV**
TEARS OF A GANGSTA I II
3X KRAZY I II
STRAIGHT BEAST MODE I II
DE'KARI
TRIGGADALE I II III
MURDAROBER WAS THE CASE I II

Elijah R. Freeman
GOD BLESS THE TRAPPERS I, II, III
THESE SCANDALOUS STREETS I, II, III
FEAR MY GANGSTA I, II, III IV, V
THESE STREETS DON'T LOVE NOBODY I, II
BURY ME A G I, II, III, IV, V
A GANGSTA'S EMPIRE I, II, III, IV
THE DOPEMAN'S BODYGAURD I II
THE REALEST KILLAZ I II III
THE LAST OF THE OGS I II III
Tranay Adams
THE STREETS ARE CALLING
Duquie Wilson
MARRIED TO A BOSS I II III
By Destiny Skai & Chris Green
KINGZ OF THE GAME I II III IV V VI VII
CRIME BOSS
Playa Ray
SLAUGHTER GANG I II III
RUTHLESS HEART I II III
By Willie Slaughter
FUK SHYT
By Blakk Diamond
DON'T F#CK WITH MY HEART I II
By Linnea
ADDICTED TO THE DRAMA I II III
IN THE ARM OF HIS BOSS II

By Jamila
YAYO I II III IV
A SHOOTER'S AMBITION I II
BRED IN THE GAME
By S. Allen
TRAP GOD I II III
RICH $AVAGE I II III
MONEY IN THE GRAVE I II III
By Martell Troublesome Bolden
FOREVER GANGSTA I II
GLOCKS ON SATIN SHEETS I II
By Adrian Dulan
TOE TAGZ I II III IV
LEVELS TO THIS SHYT I II
IT'S JUST ME AND YOU I II
By Ah'Million
KINGPIN DREAMS I II III
RAN OFF ON DA PLUG
By Paper Boi Rari
CONFESSIONS OF A GANGSTA I II III IV
CONFESSIONS OF A JACKBOY I II
By Nicholas Lock
I'M NOTHING WITHOUT HIS LOVE
SINS OF A THUG
TO THE THUG I LOVED BEFORE
A GANGSTA SAVED XMAS
IN A HUSTLER I TRUST

The Plug of Lil Mexico 2

By Monet Dragun

CAUGHT UP IN THE LIFE I II III

THE STREETS NEVER LET GO I II III

By Robert Baptiste

NEW TO THE GAME I II III

MONEY, MURDER & MEMORIES I II III

By **Malik D. Rice**

LIFE OF A SAVAGE I II III IV

A GANGSTA'S QUR'AN I II III IV

MURDA SEASON I II III

GANGLAND CARTEL I II III

CHI'RAQ GANGSTAS I II III IV

KILLERS ON ELM STREET I II III

JACK BOYZ N DA BRONX I II III

A DOPEBOY'S DREAM I II III

JACK BOYS VS DOPE BOYS I II III

COKE GIRLZ

COKE BOYS

SOSA GANG I II III

BRONX SAVAGES

BODYMORE KINGPINS

BLOOD OF A GOON

By Romell Tukes

LOYALTY AIN'T PROMISED I II

By Keith Williams

QUIET MONEY I II III

THUG LIFE I II III

Chris Green

EXTENDED CLIP I II
A GANGSTA'S PARADISE
By **Trai'Quan**
THE STREETS MADE ME I II III
By **Larry D. Wright**
THE ULTIMATE SACRIFICE I, II, III, IV, V, VI
KHADIFI
IF YOU CROSS ME ONCE I II
ANGEL I II III IV
IN THE BLINK OF AN EYE
By **Anthony Fields**
THE LIFE OF A HOOD STAR
By Ca$h & Rashia Wilson
THE STREETS WILL NEVER CLOSE I II III
By K'ajji
CREAM I II III
THE STREETS WILL TALK
By Yolanda Moore
NIGHTMARES OF A HUSTLA I II III
BLOOD AND GAMES
By King Dream
CONCRETE KILLA I II III
VICIOUS LOYALTY I II III
By Kingpen
HARD AND RUTHLESS I II
MOB TOWN 251
THE BILLIONAIRE BENTLEYS I II III

REAL G'S MOVE IN SILENCE

By Von Diesel

GHOST MOB

Stilloan Robinson

MOB TIES I II III IV V VI

SOUL OF A HUSTLER, HEART OF A KILLER I II III

GORILLAZ IN THE TRENCHES I II III

By SayNoMore

BODYMORE MURDERLAND I II III

THE BIRTH OF A GANGSTER I II

By Delmont Player

FOR THE LOVE OF A BOSS

By C. D. Blue

MOBBED UP I II III IV

THE BRICK MAN I II III IV V

THE COCAINE PRINCESS I II III IV V VI VII VIII IX

SUPER GREMLIN

By King Rio

KILLA KOUNTY I II III IV

By Khufu

MONEY GAME I II

By Smoove Dolla

A GANGSTA'S KARMA I II III

By FLAME

KING OF THE TRENCHES I II III

by **GHOST & TRANAY ADAMS**

QUEEN OF THE ZOO I II

Chris Green

By **Black Migo**
GRIMEY WAYS I II III
By Ray Vinci
XMAS WITH AN ATL SHOOTER
By Ca$h & Destiny Skai
KING KILLA
By Vincent "Vitto" Holloway
BETRAYAL OF A THUG I II
By Fre$h
THE MURDER QUEENS I II III
By Michael Gallon
TREAL LOVE
By Le'Monica Jackson
FOR THE LOVE OF BLOOD I II III
By Jamel Mitchell
HOOD CONSIGLIERE I II
By Keese
PROTÉGÉ OF A LEGEND I II III
LOVE IN THE TRENCHES
By Corey Robinson
BORN IN THE GRAVE I II III
By Self Made Tay
MOAN IN MY MOUTH
SANCTIFIED AND HORNY
By XTASY
TORN BETWEEN A GANGSTER AND A GENTLEMAN
By J-BLUNT & Miss Kim

The Plug of Lil Mexico 2

LOYALTY IS EVERYTHING I II

Molotti

HERE TODAY GONE TOMORROW

By Fly Rock

PILLOW PRINCESS

By S. Hawkins

NAÏVE TO THE STREETS

WOMEN LIE MEN LIE I II III

GIRLS FALL LIKE DOMINOS

STACK BEFORE YOU SPURLGE

FIFTY SHADES OF SNOW I II III

By A. Roy Milligan

SALUTE MY SAVAGERY

By Fumiya Payne

<u>BOOKS BY LDP'S CEO, CA$H</u>

TRUST IN NO MAN

TRUST IN NO MAN 2

TRUST IN NO MAN 3

BONDED BY BLOOD

SHORTY GOT A THUG

THUGS CRY

THUGS CRY 2

THUGS CRY 3

TRUST NO BITCH

TRUST NO BITCH 2

TRUST NO BITCH 3

TIL MY CASKET DROPS

RESTRAINING ORDER

RESTRAINING ORDER 2

IN LOVE WITH A CONVICT

LIFE OF A HOOD STAR

XMAS WITH AN ATL SHOOTER

The Plug of Lil Mexico 2